UNMASKED SEMBLANCES

17 AUTHORS. 17 ANECDOTES. 17 REASONS

SARAH EBRAHIM

First Published in 2020 by

Becomeshakespeare.com

One Point Six Technologies Pvt. Ltd.
119-123, 1st Floor, Building J2, B - Wing,
Wadala Truck Terminal, Wadala East,
Mumbai 400022, Maharashtra, INDIA
T: +91 8080226699

ISBN - 978-93-90463-33-6

UNMASKED SEMBLANCES

17 AUTHORS. 17 ANECDOTES. 17 REASONS

READ. IDEATE. INTROSPECT.

To **Kavya Ma'am,**

For mentoring and inspiring us

Always!

Musing from the Mentor's Desk

part of me wishes
that art sojourns under
your presence like spring
lilies and the soft autumn showers

a part of me,
seeks you to seek from art
the lunatic ways of life and
death

a part of me breathes
in tranquil that you've chosen
to be the change maker- a path
so full of blooming nuances

a path of grandma tales
and personal nostalgia

mix the two worlds, dear you
and create not what they expect
you to; be the artist that listens
only and only to his/her
own art

Love,
Captain Kavya

ACKNOWLEDGEMENT

We thank the Supreme one for bringing us all together in this project, for helping us in successfully completing it and for sending countless blessings our way.

Started off as a quite ordinary workshop but led 17 emerging authors to create something special and treasured. A guru-dakshina to our mentor, Kavya Sharma for mentoring us in the art of drafting out novels and stories and awakening the essence and spirit of writing within us. This book is a tribute to your guidance, your spur and your inspiration of transforming our mere, anarchic scribbles into transcendent plots and stories. Thank you, Captain Kavya!

Thanks to our amazing publisher, Become Shakespeare who believed in 17 young newbies and their passion and provided this idea, this project the utmost help possible. It is safe to say that 'Unmasked Semblances' would definitely not be possible without you.

Special shoutout goes to the designer of our simple yet classy book cover, Anna whose masterpiece is the icing on the cake. It completed this book's outlook and no one could have justified the special meaning behind this book better than her. Thank you Anna for being a significant spirit for this team and glad to have had you onboard this journey with us!

It goes without saying that without the support of family and friends on the back-end, this journey wouldn't have been an easy one at all. Without your heartfelt prayers and blessings, we wouldn't have reached such great heights so thank you!

This journey of 9 months has been quite phenomenal and unforgettable for each one of us as publishing the book was not the only thing that we learnt. Being part of a team of adept and awe-inspiring authors has definitely moulded each one of us to become better writers and most importantly, better critics of good plotlines, amazing character developments and well-structured stories. Thank you to all the authors who have made this voyage what it is today.

Thanks to our compiler, Sarah Ebrahim who stuck by us through thick and thin to build this work of art, that will be cherished by the 17 of us.

Time, Instincts, Memories, Senses and Humans, that was everything it took for us, 17 authors to come together to recreate something we learnt over the course of 30 days and Man, it has been one hell of a roller coaster ride.

STORIES YOU WILL WITNESS

BRIJESH JANI

"Let me out of this world of office memos and meeting minutes, and for just once, let me wander into the world of writing because that is where I want to be!" ~ Brijesh Jani

A Front-liner in the Pandemic Pandemonium and A Small Town guy with great big opportunities knocking at his door but Family, in the way of his passion. Still, not deterred by adversities, he has brought his passion back to life and creating an impact through his written works. Very active on the writing social platforms, he leaves no stone unturned when it comes to his passion.

Follow him on Instagram – @mightypen2020

It was a night with a bright full moon and its iridescent glow was enough to light up the surroundings. Brishna gave up all efforts to fall asleep and lay awake staring at the ceiling. Turning his head sideways, he could see the moonlight coming in through the cracks of the windows and doors of his ramshackled bedroom. Can it even be called a bedroom?! What with all the family members sleeping there because it was the only room that could be dwelled in. The other room was occupied with all the luggage each of them possessed. After getting a good glimpse of his family, he got up from his bed and walked to the threshold of his house. Very silently, he managed to open the ratty door and went out into the quiet, lonely street.

Serene milky white light of the moon gave a psychedelic feel and view to that street of his town Aleppo. Even after 3 years of ISIS' defeat in the city, the screams of devastated lives could be heard echoing down the same street he stood on. It was quite a sight for the sore eyes but alas, the street was now a place of ruins and rubbles of stone were, what was left behind.

Brishna looked at the pile of bricks, stones and cement he was living in and thought it was not much different from the neighbouring ruins that were dilapidated and scruffy in the same way. "Is ISIS the only reason I am living such a pathetic life? Or is there something else too!," a depressive thought passed through his conscience. Usually, he used to sigh over such thoughts.

But somehow, there was something different today. He didn't feel gloomy even a bit. Maybe, it was the moonlight which was affecting his senses. For the first time ever, he felt at calm and his mind was peaceful. He felt that the condition of his street and deep state of his heart were same –devastated and lonely. For the first time, the sight of the ruined street didn't cause him pain, instead, he felt at ease sitting amongst the ruins. He climbed the heap of remains of a devastated building and settled down on a stone from the building scrap. He looked up at the sky taking a deep breath.. Was that pretty moon reminding him of something? Or perhaps someone? His own voice rumbled in his mind – "Poonie, if the moon had a face, it would have been yours. No one in the world is prettier than you sweetie". He could also hear her heart-warming laugh in answer, sweet and lovely like a wind chime. This remembrance brought a smile on his face for a while. With a deep breath, he plunged into the ocean of those lovely memories…………

The city was not the same, the street was not the same, and most definitely his life was not the same a few years ago. Those wonder years of adolescence were the dreamiest, happiest time he had ever had. There was no civil war, no ISIS and absolutely no miseries in the life of the people of Aleppo. Aleppo was alive and happening at that time, so was his street. He firmly believed that his street was the best place to live in the entire world. Nothing less than heaven! The presence of Pooneh enlivened the street for Brishna. He felt that his entire existence revolved around Pooneh. Now who is Pooneh, one might ask!

None of the words could even justify her description. Fairy - that is what he thought her to be because how can a mortal be so beautiful and innocent. "There is no doubt that, yes, I must have done something too good to be blessed with Pooneh", he used to always ponder.

"Poonie, boys of this area as well as other parts of the city are crazy for you but you only hang out with me...Why is that so?", Brishna used to ask his dream girl. She laughed every time, blushing a little and replied, "Because you are special to me." while pulling his cheeks. Brishna loved to see her laugh and was mesmerized by the sound of her laugh. The surroundings were long forgotten whenever he talked to her.

The sound of growling broke his flood of memories and he saw that a dog was responsible for it. As soon as, Brishna threw a stone at the dog, he ran away, whining in anger and disappeared behind the shambled house at the end of the long street.

Pooneh's House!

Just by glancing at the house, all the memories came rushing back to him and he slipped again into the flashback mode. How could he forget it? Can anyone forget the wonderful days? Especially the day, when Pooneh called out for him, making it public notice.

"Brishu! Hurry up! I want you to see something", she yelled from the balcony while he was passing by (Well, actually he passed by the house the sixth time that day just in hopes to have a glance of Pooneh).

Brishna's cheeks turned red as the prettiest girl in the city called him Brishu out-front and this had caught the attention of every passer-by. Not only, did she call out his name but she also invited him to her house. With a rapidly beating heart, he responded to her, "Yes....ok....but what-" Before he could ask her anything, she cut him off by yelling in a sweet voice, "Just come fast please...."

Brishna was stumped by her request and was in a dilemma. On hearing her scream his name continuously making everyone look at him, he had no choice other than to rush into her house. Now there wasn't any chance he could let his brain intervene when his heart was sensing serendipity. But before he met her, he was stopped by Pooneh's Abbu on the staircase.

"Oye Brishna, what do you think of yourself?", he asked in a scolding voice.

Brishna, pale from fear, responded, "No....No...I.....I.... actually....."

Her father cut him off and asked, "Why did you make Pooneh yell? She has got a new iPad and wants to show it to you. Just go fast. Make sure to help her operate that stuff as none of us are educated enough to do so."

Brishna could breathe now in relief and said, "Yes... Yes... Of course uncle..." Moving hurriedly upstairs, he saw Pooneh grinning at him. Pooneh dragged him inside the room and closed the door while imitating his fumbled response to her Abbu and laughed out loud. Brishna blushed and felt excited as she was still holding onto his hand.

"Poonie...", he started to say. But Pooneh stopped him by saying, "What Poonie, huh?? When I was calling, you were still thinking and asking questions. Don't you trust me? When Abbu ordered you to help me and listen to me, you immediately obeyed him" She smiled and looked into his eyes. Dancing her eyebrows, she teased him, " I think, you like Abbu more than me."

Brishna could not breathe then. Pooneh was so close that even if any of them moved an inch ahead, they would be kissing each other. Her soft, perfectly shaped body, her mesmerizing sweet fragrance, untied hair, sight of her cleavage peeping and smooth fair skin.... everything was driving him crazy.

"Should I take a chance and kiss?", Brishna thought but felt guilty and lost courage.

His lips trembled, "Poonie....actually....actually I Iike you more than anyone in the world... in fact...I .....I...." Pooneh again giggled while imitating his style, "I.......I....." and laughed again. "Malik al Muluk, it seems that I have to teach you alphabets again. J comes after I." Brishna too broke into a laugh. Both laughed for a long time, holding each other's hands. He felt that if there is any damn thing in the world known as love, THIS IS IT. And it's too damn beautiful and pure.

"Okay, now let's see your iPad.", he said coming back to his senses. "Idiot! Ipad was just a fake reason I gave to Abbu to call you here", she winked. His excitement again reached a new peak. She had never been so close to him before. He thought perhaps she is going to propose to him today.

"Yes man, get ready for the moment..", he said to himself. He was fully excited and aroused. "Oh damn, my mouth will stink when we kiss. I had onion Omelette for breakfast!", he thought and mentally scolded himself for not being ready.

"Oh, then why am I here??", he responded with great efforts, trying to hide his excitement.

"See this!", she excitedly squealed while removing her full-length coat and discarded it on the bed.

"Ah damn!" Brishna's jaws dropped down. She was wearing a short dress inside the coat. It was a kind of a western dress that was banned for girls in Aleppo because it was obscenely revealing. "How do I look?", she asked dancing her eyebrows and took a spin on her heels with both hands raised like a ballet dancer.

Brishna was staring madly at her angelic beauty and grace. Her milky white thighs, smooth glistening shoulders, glabrate armpits, skimpily clad and prominent rounded hips. All these had managed to get him transfixed as he was not the one to have been in this situation before. His excitement broke all barriers and his breath rushed faster than before. Not only did his lungs fill with air faster but also, his heart was beating so fast that he felt as if it will come out of his chest. He tried to utter a few words but he was a complete mess! Woah, he wanted to hug her so tight and whisper sweet nothings into her ear "I love you Poonie" while kissing every part of her silky smooth body.

He could see her saying something but he was so excited that he was mentally not there to apprehend what she was saying and at that moment, he plucked up the courage to tell her how he felt. He moved towards her and held both her hands with his one hand and put his second hand on her waist pulling her close to him. Surprise was the only plausible emotion Pooneh was going through. But before any of them could say anything, there was a knock on the door.

All the fizz of excitement disappeared and the beautiful moment had been ruined. He didn't know what to do. But before he could react, Pooneh had already opened the door and dragged the visitor inside and made sure to close it again. Younger siblings are sure a menace because in our case it was Doa, Pooneh's younger sister. Brishna took a breath of relief knowing that it could have been Pooneh's Abbu but also knew that now chances of proposing and kissing Pooneh had been washed down the drain.

"Brishna, see her amazing dress. She is like a Hollywood staaaar. Doesn't she look great?", Doa asked him. "Well..... that's ....that's amazing and she is looking damn hot in it. I am going crazy Doa. Your sis is truly a *fairy*! ", he gathered courage and spoke his mind. Both sisters laughed giving high five to each other. "But how did you manage to get it?", he asked. Both sisters stopped laughing and put on their serious faces. They both glanced at each other and again burst into a laugh.

"Brishnaaaaa....." his mother's voice broke his dreamy trance and the flashback train he had boarded and he realized that it's almost morning. "Get ready dear. Mr. George will be coming", mother said.

It was a little hard for Brishna to come back to the present. He wanted to stay in the treasure of hedonistic memories a bit longer. But at the same time, he was also quite aware that dealing well with Mr George was extremely crucial at this juncture. Unwillingly, he got up from the stone and moved inside the house. When he came back after a bath, he saw that his mom had kept his breakfast ready. He sat and started eating without looking at her. He feared his mother might read his eyes. What he wasn't aware of, was that his mother had already sensed his mental state. "When your father passed away, I had two choices. One was to succumb to depression and negativity, live life cursing myself and the world. Second it being was to hand over all your four siblings to any of our relatives, get married to someone and start a new life.", she spoke in one breath while serving him another omelette, pausing for a second to gauge his reaction. She saw that Brishna froze for a while and stopped eating. She knew that her son was all ears now. She continued while serving the sauce on his plate, "But my Mom encouraged me otherwise so I chose to live happily *for and with* the ones I love. You, *four*, Brishna. You and your siblings! And it was easy once I decided. Today I am proud that I chose wisely. Allah has been protecting us! Although we couldn't leave this place like others did in times of the Caliphate attempts. But we survived those darkest days and scariest nights! And today, the eldest male in our family, Brishna, is now going to embark upon a new journey with affluent Mr George's company. Proud of you Brishna for taking responsibility of the family so well!"

The words had already casted a spell on Brishna. He was all ears and even forgot to blink for a while. The mom he could see that day, was a different person altogether! "Remember, either we can let situations design our destiny or we can take control and choose to pave the paths to our destiny our own way", she completed and went away. Brishna was stunned. He never stopped to think about the struggles that his mother had to live through. He had noticed the wrinkles on her face but he never thought about her emotional state all these years. He felt quite embarrassed.

"Taste that hummus. Sabr has made it for you." Mother said while going out for fetching water. It again spoiled his mood. "Why is Sabr even bothering to do all of this? Can't she see that I am simply not interested in her? She is not even half pretty compared to Pooneh.", he said to himself. Brishna then, got angry with himself that he couldn't stop memories of Pooneh again flooding his mind and he was back on the flashback train.

That day, Doa came with sweets to his home. She gave a box of sweets to his mom and said that this was for Pooneh's engagement. She knew Brishna was there and without even looking at him, she ran away hurriedly. Brishna thought it was a sort of practical joke being played on him but sheer anxiety took the best of him so he rushed to Pooneh's home. Pooneh was alone. "Hey Brishu..." she immediately responded. She seemed to be shying away from him . Before Brishna could ask her anything, she put a sweet in his mouth and said "This is the last time. Now I will be someone's wife."

Brishna was shocked. He was severely frustrated and angry. He grabbed both her shoulders and shook her fiercely. "Then what about us Poonie? How could you think of marrying someone?", he cried. She gently pushed him away and said, "What are you talking about, Brishna? Are you kidding? You are like my brother. I have never looked at you that way!" "STOP!", he yelled and continued to say, "Brother?? Did either of us EVER mention that we are brother and sister?" She quickly replied, "Did either of us EVER say that we love each other or will marry?" Brishna cursed himself for not proposing to her at the right time. He had no answer. He tried to put his point, "But.... but... I...I love you..." "Please understand Brishu, I always wanted to marry someone from my own caste and finally, I am so elated today. Even my parents are happy today. Allah knows, why you aren't happy! Listen, forget everything and consider the time spent together as time-pass. You know that we will always be best friends. You will find a better girl and –"

The rally of memories could have lasted longer if an unknown voice had not broken the trance and brought him back to the present. "Excuse me, is this Mr. Brishna Abdel?", a man in a white uniform knocked the ratty door and asked politely. It took a moment for Brishna to connect back with his present. He nodded affirmatively. Although he didn't like an interruption in his thoughts but kept his facial expressions polite.

"Mr. George has sent this. It's your first assignment of the job", the chauffer said giving him an envelope. Brishna opened it after the chauffeur left and started reading the letter.

***

Brishna had never been to Istanbul before and also, never had a chance to fly. He was happy and excited during the flight that finally his life was on track. After all, how many get such a job that gives opportunity of international travels at company's cost. "I will make Mr. George proud", he promised himself. He felt that he has experienced this level of excitement after many years. Perhaps, first time after his tryst with Pooneh. The flight was about to land. The sight of

Istanbul's evening from the sky was so pleasurable that he forgot everything else for a while.

Later in the day, around 7.30 in the evening, Brishna had entered the golden banquet hall as per instructions of the assignment given to him. The most prestigious banquet hall of Istanbul was witnessing a special party being hosted by the wealthiest person of Turkey – Alim Demir.

Brishna was wearing an Indian style outfit as the dress code for the gathering was Indian ethnic. His mission was to get snaps of Turkish business tycoon's arrogant and inaccessible wife. No one from the media had her photos. The hall was full of elite class people and no one from the media was allowed to have cameras but this was no issue to worry on for Brishna as he was given the identity of a socialite and he was going to click photos with a hidden camera. He was standing near the doorway and surveying the golden banquet hall, which was filled with refined bodies in saris and jackets, and beautiful young women.

And the moment came!

Business tycoon Alim Demir entered the hall with his spouse. He was surrounded by associates and bodyguards. Demir couple was hardly visible. He slowly and carefully moved towards them. It was paramount that no one got to know his intentions. He could see the back of a gorgeous woman with straight hairs in sleeveless blouse and saree holding the hand of Alim Demir. "Damn these business tycoons. They always manage to get wives much more beautiful and younger than them", he thought. He moved closer to them, very slowly keeping his eyes on Mrs. Demir. If she turned back, he was ready to capture her snap with a hidden button camera.

From behind, she reminded him of his love – Pooneh, for a moment. But he forcefully pushed the thoughts away to concentrate on the mission. And cursed himself for not being able to get rid of his thoughts that revolved around Pooneh. He shook his head a little and moved a bit ahead to concentrate on the *subject*. Now he was very close to the group surrounding the couple. He was ready with the gadgets to take snaps at any moment and the couple turned back. He immediately clicked the button of the device in his pocket. The next second was a blur because the only emotion that raced through him was of shock and he couldn't click further. She was Pooneh. *His dream girl* Pooneh! He rubbed his eyes and shook his head. But no, his eyes weren't betraying him. Excitement of seeing her, not in dreams or flashbacks but in reality, overpowered the resentment. He couldn't withhold his outburst and screamed – "Poonieee...."

He was so loud that it drew everyone's attention towards him. Alim seemed angry and the ambience was tense as the people could see his wife anxious. No one had seen any expression on her face during any public event. Alim gave an inkling to his bodyguard and they moved towards Brishna. Immediately, Pooneh whispered something in her husband's ears and Alim called back his bodyguards the very next moment. Demir couple moved ahead with the group without even looking at Brishna, as if nothing had happened. And the party was rocking again! As if everyone had forgotten Brishna's existence in the hall. Brishna couldn't understand what happened. He was about to call her again when he felt a tight grip on his shoulder. The cruel looking man cued him to stay silent and come with him. That man's cruel face brought Brishna back to reality and he thought it was advisable to follow his instructions. He took Brishna to a room away from the gathering, pushed him inside and closed the door from the outside. Pooneh was waiting for him in the room. Anger was spilling from every curve and corner of her beautiful body. But before Brishna could speak, she rambled in a frustrated voice, "I thought you were dead in the civil war. Why did you come here and why did you call me in front of everyone? I am married now. Don't you understand?"

"But you said, you had married in your caste. Caste, my foot! Alim is not even of your age. Didn't you know I loved you deeply? You are the dream of my life, Poonie! Why did you dump me? And if you were not interested then why did you get so close in the first place?", Brishna couldn't stop crying while trying to converse. "Please stop this nonsense!", she yelled at Brishna for the first time in her life. "Listen, Alim belongs to the most respectable caste in the world. And it's called 'The Billionaires' Club'. Any girl would get married from *this caste*. When a wretched lad like you can dream of having *ME*, don't you think a beauty like me deserves to live her dream life?"

She couldn't sympathize with the tears flooding from Brishna's eyes. Instead, his crying and sobbing infuriated her even more. "Brishna, you could never realize that wealth is the only thing that matters for girls. I couldn't have spend my life in stone broke streets of Aleppo. So, I chose Alim. I am his youngest and dearest wife. And yes, everyone needs a friend of their age which I didn't have. You were the only person of my age group in the entire locality. That's it! I never ever thought of you as my beau!", she spoke an untold truth out of outburst of anger. Brishna was shocked to death by her words. The very next moment, she felt a bit bad for being so harsh towards Brishna who continued to sob over his fate.

She raised his chin with her hand and said politely, "Please understand. I beg you to leave me alone. I am someone's wife now. I have a life to live!" And without awaiting his response, she clapped. A cruel-looking bouncer opened the doors and got inside to take Brishna away. Brishna was still in awe of the wounds by his dream girl's stinging words. But he also felt deep bliss when she touched his chin. That moment of bliss felt like a blessing to Brishna. It was like quenching your thirst after wandering hours and hours in the torrid barren desert. The cruel faced hunk grabbed his shoulder and pushed him. Brishna recovered fast, sensing the situation to be convenient. He wiped his tears and said, "Ok. I'll leave.... But can I see your dazzling smile that I have always craved and cherished? Please! It has been seven years since your family left *Syria* and I can't get rid of your thoughts as you have consumed my senses. I love you and always wanted to see you smile. Please, for my love's sake!"

She thought it was okay to extend such a tiny favor to this nerk lover. And she smiled. It was the same dazzling smile that Brishna always craved to see. "She has grown more beautiful than before.", Brishna felt for a while but he controlled his emotions the very next moment. As promised, he turned back with tears and left. He was taken directly outside without entering the hall. Brishna took a cab to go to the airport. He wiped his tears and burst into a laugh. He dialled George's number and said, "Mission accomplished, sir. I got her snaps. Smiling ones too. And guess what, we will be the first newspaper to have her *so far* hidden history. And a video confessing it all." George apparently sounded extremely happy.

"The most respected caste in the world is 'The Billionaires' Club'!", he murmured and repeated the words his dream girl had reiterated today, remembering the biggest lesson of his life. "See you in the club soon dear Poonie, *youngest and dearest wife* of Mr. Alim! Be ready to welcome me", he murmured while watching footage recorded by his secret button camera. His cab was entering the airport premises where he made the second call to his mother.

"Ammi, I am returning in the morning. Please ask Sabr to keep hummus ready for me. Tell her that I have requested her to make it."

PARIJAT SARKAR

"I write what I believe in. I won't write a story that I haven't experienced personally or passively." ~ Parijat

A Supermom whose superpower entails the ability to write works that engender empathy and understanding on the part of each reader. Poetry enthusiast who fortes in tragedy and drama fiction but yearns to try a hand at Fantasy too. Simple captions with thought-provoking musings are her stratagems in the field of writing.

Follow her on Instagram - @only_parijat

It was a pleasant and calm evening even though the sun had retired to its resting room and the sky was a still bright orange hue. Birds were flying back to their homes, chattering amongst themselves. But, unlike her neighbours who were enjoying their evening tea, Niti did not have enough time to breathe. She had been busy the whole day, preparing for her son's birthday.

Her son had gone to her in-law's house last night. He was supposedly coming back in a few hours or so and Niti wanted to give him a surprise. Except she forgot how extremely time-consuming the task was. Plenty of people were attending the party. She had no idea how she was going to organize it all by herself.

Yesterday, she even asked her husband if he could get hold of a cook or even a kitchen helper for her. But he said that he could not find anyone to help her on such short notice. She had asked a bunch of people, her relatives in town. But no one was free. Everyone either had plans or somewhere to go to. And that's not even the worst part. Considering all her relatives had plans, their presence at the party was highly unlikely. And she also knew that they were narrating premeditated fibs.

For instance, her mother-in-law outright denied to show up at the party. Because she, being a member of the "Ladies Society", seemingly had a very crucial meeting that could not be postponed for anything. What could be more important than her own grandson's birthday party! Especially, since she was not even their president anymore. She quit six months ago, due to some mysterious reason. Then there was her father-in-law who had no trouble walking to the market on his own but could not come to the party because he had severe joint pain in presumably his whole body. Buaji was going to her daughter's house, mamaji was on a vacation.

All the other relatives aside, who she didn't care for all that much, her mother-in-law's refusal truly hurt her. She was the closest person to Niti after her husband, Suhas. After all, Niti had no contact with her own mother or anyone from her own family.

***

"Is that why we sent you to that expensive college? So that you can go out with every guy you want to? Especially a non-brahmin boy?", her father spat in her face while her mother kept silently weeping in a corner. "We hold our culture with such high regards and you have the audacity to stand in front of me and declare your love for that lowlife! How dare you!"

"But Papa, he is a good-" her father did not let her finish.

"I don't want to listen to a word you have to say!", her father thundered, "I have listened enough. Letting you go to that college was my biggest mistake. Our ancestors were right. Girls of your age should be looking after their kids at home. But I'm a moron that let you walk all over me. But it won't happen again." Then he turned his back on her and what he told her then, seemed like multiple slaps to her face. "You have to choose, Niti! Your family or that scoundrel. If you do choose that scum then don't bother coming back here. Consider your parents dead. And we will think that our daughter has committed suicide.

***

That was the last interaction she had with her family. At that time, Niti, homeless and destitute, turned to Suhas. But his grandfather, the head of the family, denied to let her stay with them if they were not married. Out of obligation, Suhas proposed marriage to her. Niti, troubled that her future plans of studying higher and obtaining employment would be wrecked so she wanted to reject his offer. But Suhas assured her that he would tend to her higher education and assist her to procure a job. Hence, Niti somewhat reluctantly agreed to the marriage.

Within a few months, they got hitched and they moved to where Suhas' family business was placed. But with this shift, all her hopes and aspirations seemed to have left her, all her dreams were crushed. Suhas had conveniently forgotten about his promises to her. And day by day as he became more and more involved with his job, he started spending less and less time at home. She was trapped in the house, she was lonely and exhausted. She went about her day in the confinements of her house, feeling fully drained.

One day, suddenly her mother-in-law came to visit and saw her and immediately knew something was wrong with her. Mrs. Ray tried to talk to her and console her. And when she finally understood Niti's problem, she even asked her to join in the " Ladies Society". But she did not want to. It was awfully odd that even though she felt caged, at the same time she didn't want to leave the cell. She didn't feel a fraction of the girl she used to be in college. Mrs. Ray was the only person who would come to check on her and occasionally spend some time with her. They became as close as possible.

Yet, she couldn't let go of the empty feeling in her chest. But her agonies came to an end.

On the 22nd of July, 2010, Soham was born. That was the day her whole life changed for the better. At first, she did not feel the connection with him that a mother and her child should have. And that scared her for a moment.

"Have I become numb?", she thought to herself, "Am I dead from the inside? Is that why I don't feel any connection with my son?"

But soon all her doubts were washed away when Soham opened his beautiful big brown eyes for the very first time and stared at her. She could feel the rock that she had been harbouring in her innermost part, melting away. Her heart was swelling with adoration, her whole existence had turned brighter. And that was the day she made her son her mission, her one true love.

Soham was the sunshine of her life and every day, she woke up to greet the light that gave her, her purpose of existence.

When Soham grinned at her for the first time, not just his unintentional sleepy smile, but actually gave her his toothless-simper, the happiness she felt was not comparable to anything. When he called her 'ma' for the first time, her heart burst with joy. When he first started walking, she sobbed.

Every time, he cried just for her attention, she hugged him feeling a sense of peace, of tranquillity, a soothing sensation to her aching heart. As Soham was growing up, Niti's love for him kept growing.

They used to play hide and seek. Niti pretended to look for him and then ultimately 'found' him after which the tickling war started and Soham was a giggling mess, clutching onto his stomach, rolling on the floor with Niti, was a normal occurrence in their household. Not only was he her sun, but his days also revolved around her.

Sometimes, they often danced together to whatever song was on the radio. Both of them knew that they were hilariously bad. So then they laughed it off. Soham's favourite place was their back yard. There, he and his Ma played cricket together. She was not particularly good at the game, but he had a lot of fun winning almost every time they played.

But his favourite time was when he came back home from school. His mother was always standing by the gate, ready to welcome him with open arms and give him a bear hug. And, after he had changed from his uniform, they would goof off on the trunk of the giant mango tree they had in the backyard, for as long as they wanted, till he had to go do his homework. Or when he shared with her everything he did in class that day. Or when he swayed from the tire-swing hanging from one of the branches of the mango tree. His mother never reprimanded him but he knew that she was always worried that he would fall from the tire. These were minor and modest moments that he cherished greatly.

Sometimes he played on the computer for too long and his mother would rebuke him. Then he would pout at her and she'd just forget that she was ever mad at him.

He liked to aggravate her a little bit too much. He would steal sweets from the kitchen when his mother was busy cooking.

He tried to climb up the mango tree once, just to frighten his mother. He loved it when he could just conceal something that she needed promptly and when she was unable to find it, he dangled it in front of her face and then fled the scene with the object in question in his hand.

Despite everything, she seldom got really angry with him. She was his best friend. His mother was the one who taught him cycling. She was the one who taught him anything actually.

Then there were things that they did for the heck of it. Every so often, he would run down to her and give her a hug or a kiss on the cheeks. Occasionally, she would give him piggyback rides for no apparent reason.

People preferred to say that Niti was obsessed with her son to some extent, obnoxiously. Her love was the grapevine that made Soham its support. But she never paid any heed to those gossiping uncles and aunts. The same people who implicitly declined her invitation to Soham's birthday party. But, still, there were a few folks coming. There was Suhas' colleagues, their neighbours. Suhas volunteered to invite them. He was also supposed to bring the cake and the confetti and party hats and all the confectionery he could find. But he was not there yet. He was late. He should have been home by 5:30 PM. If he was home he could help her out with the preparation. That is why she wanted a helper.

A few months ago Niti was sick. So Suhas brought a woman home one day. He told Niti, "She will help you with your household chores."

But Niti never liked that woman. More often than not she acted bossy and it was not appreciated by Niti at all. So, occasionally Niti would lash out at her though she felt terrible about it afterwards. Sometimes she would give Niti medicines that made her dopey. Thus Niti wanted her gone as soon as possible. Suhas was completely against it. But he eventually came around it. So they let her go. Likewise, someone else came. But Niti had problems with this one too. Then another one came, then another one.

After letting go of the seventh one, Suhas finally had enough. He said he would not bring anyone else. He was immensely annoyed. Maybe that was the reason that he didn't bring any helper for her when she asked him yesterday.

At a quarter past six, Suhas reached home. He was in a blue full-sleeved shirt and grey pants. He slowly entered the house. He was slightly hunched, his steps were heavy. He wanted to sit down on the chair in front of him, but he knew that he couldn't.

He looked straight at the kitchen and saw his wife wearing a saree with the aanchal tucked in her hip. She was cooking something. He stayed that way for a few minutes, looking at her until she saw him. She smiled at him and then asked, "Where have you been? I thought you will come home early and help me with the party. Did you invite everyone?"

He didn't say anything just kept looking at her with tenderness in his eyes. At the lack of response from him, she grew a little bit nervous. So she asked again, "You did invite everyone, right? You didn't forget, right?", then took a glance behind him and again asked, "Where is the cake and everything that I asked you to bring?"

He took a deep breath and then said, "Just… do whatever you were doing. Everything will be fine. I'm going to the backyard. I need fresh air." Niti frowned a little bit but didn't comment on it and went about her work.

Upon entering the backyard, Suhas saw that the sky had turned dark but the lights were still off. He searched for the switchboard and flipped it on. He stared at the lawn. The grass was neatly cut. It was clean, except for a few leaves that had fallen from the mango tree. Nothing seemed to be out of place. Except for everything was.

It was ridiculous, really. Suhas never thought his life could take this turn.

Everything in his life was designed by either his family or himself. He was the good boy of the family. Everything they told him to do, he did without complaining. The only time he did anything without his parents' permission was when he fell in love with Niti.

When he met her, Niti was just in her first year of college, an ever-smiling, invigorating, animated woman. By the third year, they were inseparable. When this news reached his home, his parents thought that it was just an affair and soon it would be over. But it never did.

So his grandfather, who was the patriarch of the family, struck a deal with him. He had to marry Niti right after his graduation, otherwise, he was not about to give Suhas a dime.

There were two motives behind this demand. Firstly, they did not want people to find out that Suhas was in a relationship before marriage, that's just embarrassing. Secondly, they wanted her to be solely dedicated to her home. They wanted her to be a perfect housewife. But she was independent and fierce. Everyone knew that once she finished college, she was going to go places. Then it would be impossible to get his family's blessing.

So he did what he thought was appropriate. He asked Niti to marry him. Niti was hesitant to say yes at first. But after a lot of persuasion and promises, albeit false, Niti finally agreed and shortly after she passed out of college, they got married. He was over the moon at first, but his joy was short-lived.

A few days later, an overwhelming sense of guilt overcame him. He was actively deceiving his wife. He was never going to keep his promise.

After they got married and moved into their new home he could see how frightfully disheartened she was. It pained him to see her like that. Being overpowered by this ache, a few months later, he went behind everyone's back and offered her a job in his company. She rejected it.

It truly hurt him. He didn't know why she'd do that. He knew that she was depressed, she was the one who was betrayed. But it still hurt. He was swallowed by guilt again, which in turn made him angry. He was angry at Niti, he was angry at his grandfather, but most of all he was disappointed at himself. He should've never married her. He knew she would never be happy in her purgatory, they called home. But he still insisted and pressurized her to marry him.

As months passed, he kept looking at her, withering away, a ghost of the person he fell in love with. She was not her cheerful, brilliant-self anymore, and Suhas knew that it was his fault. His conscience kept eating him alive.

Suhas, badly beaten and bruised by his life and decisions turned to work excessively to stay away from home.

When Soham was born, he finally saw glimpses of his old college lover, he was a little bit relieved. But he was already too engulfed in his guilt to be homebound and look at Niti, anymore.

Every day, he woke up before Niti and went to his office before she stirred from her slumber. Then he would go back home late when he knew that Niti would be asleep by then. All of this to ensure that he never had to look Niti in the eyes. It was not like she knew that he was sneaking in and out of his own house, anyway. She was too busy with Soham. He knew that it sounded childish and egotistical, but he sometimes wished that she would show him a fraction of the love and care she had for Soham. But he also knew that deep down she resented him.

He peered at the kitchen and saw that his wife was searching frantically for something in the cabinets. He sighed and looked at his right. There laid Soham's bicycle by the trunk of the mango tree. He stared at it with almost a wistful look in his eyes. He touched it delicately. Even after repairing it extensively it still had a few dents, few scratches here and there.

He then sat down with his back to the tree-trunk. He caught sight of the tire-swing and shoved it slightly. He had a faraway look in his eyes like he was beholding a ten-year-old boy sitting there and giggling at him, coaxing him to push more. He gulped the painful ball of thorn stuck in his throat.

"You know, your mom is organizing your birthday party. Again. Everyday she makes enough food to feed a village. Now I have a new task. Every night after your Ma falls asleep, I go out to seek street-kids and feed them the excess food every night", he said ruefully.

"At first, I thought that I would be okay with it. But it has continued to be more and more hurtful. I want to take care of her but she has become increasingly inconsolable. Every night I have to make up some lie, tell her why you can't come home tonight, every night. Every night, I drag her down to the bed and make her take the sleep medication. I appointed a few nurses. But she doesn't listen to anyone. She was physically violent with them. I had to let them go. You have to believe me when I say that I tried. I really tried to take care of her. But I failed.", he started tearing up but he wiped them with the hem of his shirt. He remembered his promise he made to his son.

***

6 months ago

Suhas unlocked the front door with his spear keys and went in. The living room was dimly lit with a bulb over the front door and a lamp by the sofa. Worn out, he sat down on the sofa, neglecting to turn the fan on. The temperature inside was decent so he let it be. He was about to get up when Soham came down the stairs. He was a little bit frightened to see his father on the sofa. But when realization dawned on him, he smiled his cheeky smile and went to sit beside him.

"Hey, Pa!", Soham said to him.

"Hey, Somu.", he replied, smiling slightly.

"Pa you forgot something today."

"What?"

"That today is Saturday,", Soham said, "and your not supposed to go to the office today."

"I had a really important meeting today, Somu. I had to go.", Suhas sighed.

"Yeah, but you said you will take us out for dinner.", he said sitting straight and crossing his hands above his chest with a hint of annoyance in his voice.

Suhas sat straight up and looked at Soham with a horrid expression on his face. "Fff... fish! I'm so sorry Somu! I totally forgot!", he said with a pleading tone.

"You know, I know you were going to say the 'f' word. And you never take us anywhere. Last time, we went out two years ago on your business trip. You were never with us. It was just me and ma. It felt like it."

"I'm so so sorry Somu. It will never happen ever again."

Soham continued with a pout on his face, "You never spend any time with us, ever. You never go to my school functions or meetings. Ma goes everywhere alone. That's why Riddhi aunty was saying those nasty things to Ma."

"Who is Riddhi and what was she saying?", Suhas asked, creasing his brow.

"She is my friend, Anuj's mother. And she was saying that you are cheating on Maa."

"What!" Suhas was livid. But then, a few seconds later, he deflated.

He looked at his son. Soham was growing up, fast. His shaggy hair was slumping on his forehead. He needed a haircut. The last of his baby fat was melting away from his face. His jaw was hardening. He was looking down as if he was ashamed of his father. Suhas never knew that Soham had the ability to even understand what 'cheating' meant.

He took both of Soham's hands in his unusually large hands and squeezed lightly. "Somu don't ever believe anything like that. You and your Ma are my first and last love." Besides he was guilty enough, he did not want the additional burden of infidelity.

"Then promise me that you will spend more time with us. You don't know Pa but I know that Ma misses you. Promise me that you will take care of her."

"I promise. Tell you what, next week is your birthday. So, the day after your birthday, we will go for a picnic." Suhas said smiling.

"Yea!"

That's when Niti also came down.

"What are you two doing here so late?"

"We're just talking Ma."

"What are you doing up Somu. I thought that you were asleep.", she enquired.

"I-I, just came down to drink some water."

"Nope. You were not.", Niti said knowingly. "You just came to eat the ice cream, didn't you?"

"No no, I didn't."

"Yeah sure." Then she looked at Suhas and said, "I suppose you had dinner at the office."

"Yeah, I did."

"Okay. And Somu, no more ice cream for you tonight. You had enough. Come on. Go to bed now!"

***

"I tried to keep my promise but I couldn't. I couldn't even take you out for the picnic I promised.

"I understand, the doctors said that it will come as a big shock for her. But why can't she realize that you're…" and he choked. He was completely sobbing by then. Tears were coming out of his eyes unapologetically. Water was coming from his nose. He tried to wipe them away resulting in them being smeared in his cheek. But he continued, he had to.

"That you're never coming back to us. I… I can't take it anymore. So I'm doing it. It's my…my last resort. The doctors suggested it to me months ago. But if I did it then I would be entirely alone. I-I don't want to be alone. But I can't take it anymore. So I'm sending her away."

He was clutching his chest with his left hand. He could feel an invisible palm squashing his heart inside his ribs. But he kept going on, "They are coming in a few minutes to take her away from me. I'm so afraid, Beta. I'm scared."

As he heard a car pull up in front of the house, he looked up towards where the front gate would be. His eyes widened fearfully. He flung his body towards the tire-swing and clung to it as his life depended on it.

On the other side of the house, a few people were knocking on the door. While Niti went to the door, quietly mumbling and grumbling to herself of how she was still unprepared, Suhas on the other side was relentlessly saying, "I am sorry. I'm sorry. I'm so so sorry…"

PRABHJYOT SINGH

"I'm just trying to express the inexpressible by hiding the complexity and presenting simplicity!" ~ **Prabhjyot Singh**

A child prodigy, who sold his first software product in his teens and achieved many accolades to his name. A Hobbyist Writer and A Serial Entrepreneur, who loves to bring that idiosyncratic touch to his writings and leave his readers wanting more.

Follow him on Instagram - @prabhjyotsingh

I'm still figuring out while sitting at the dank and lonely end of this rusty old excuse for a cafe that how can someone in this time and age ruin a cup of coffee? Isn't the coffee machine supposed to do everything for you? And is finding some reasonably good coffee beans that tough a task? Or Just that expensive?

Nodding my head in anguish, I once again looked up at the waiter diagonally across from where I was seated and in that moment, the door opposite to the millennial waiter in the ripped apron, opened and an angel from the deep bosom of the heavens stepped into the cafe - rejuvenating the creaking floor boards, the foul air inside the almost dying walls and breathing life in the faces of everyone sitting there including me. With every step, she took towards the now wide-eyed, in-awe lonely waiter who seemed to have been reincarnated as an aspiring and energetic Generation Z, everyone sat transfixed by the angelic aura around her.

I realized that I was staring at her like a child watching the snowfall for the first time on his mitten covered hands. I brought myself back to this new reality and composed myself and took a sip of the not-so-bad coffee in my hands, my taste-buds no longer cursing the black liquid going to my throat.

The girl by now had found herself a seat on the side of the cafe opposite to me, and the knocked-out server now rushing himself to her table in a seemingly not so subtle way. After giving her order, she was staring outside the window at the dull parking lot as if deciding whether the parking lot deserves a little pulse of her youthful exuberance.

End of part 1

Watching her watch a mother and her daughter intently as they were headed to their car, the server was just hovering over her even after he had received his *orders* from the angelic beauty. I couldn't help but feel bad for the waiter that he no longer had control over his body; it was as if he was no longer in this reality, like he no longer wanted to be *just* a waiter, it was as if his dreams no longer had bounds and he was struggling to find the right words that wouldn't be construed as blasphemy.

The vibration brought my focus back to myself and I glanced left towards the screen to see who was calling me and with a sigh, I realized that I just had enough time to come to this cafe and get a cup of coffee and rush over to the St Andrews station to be there just in time to catch the 06:55pm to my friend's place. It was supposed to be me and Andy going over to Jen's place for the Thanksgiving dinner.

Oh! I hate this dilemma, should I ignore the call and bathe in this unearthly aurora? or somehow drag myself out and head to the metro station? The Gen-Z by now is back at his rightful place behind the counter making a fresh pot of the black liquid that he had the guts to call coffee, I mean why even bother brewing it? His face contorted as he silently shouted curses - watching the way he's working and not focusing on the task at hand, I assumed that his brain and tongue coordination failed at the worst possible time.

"Hey Andy!

Yeah I'm just grabbing a cup of coffee.

At Nick's

Yeah I'm running a bit late, I'll catch the next one and be there by 8.

Great, see ya there."

So much for my dilemma, it was as if I was in a trance doing what my master wanted me to do and as if on command I looked up again at her and noticed her looking right back at me.

End of part 2

I froze; my mind wandering the depths of the universe, running a million simulations per second in order to find the best way to react to her Godly gaze. It was as if everything had slowed down for me and was made *clearer*, and she was still looking right at me. I gave her a nod as I would to any other stranger I meet on the road and in lieu of the friendly-nod that I expected in return, I could see anxiety in her eyes. My reflex reaction to go to her was suppressed by my sanity and I decided to observe the situation more.

She had begun scanning the faces of everyone coming through the surprisingly silent doors of this almost forgotten coffee shop, her anxiety now apparent from her body language, her legs shaking, her eyes wandering the cafe, looking for something in the faces of the patrons from the perfect vantage point that was her table.

She looked away and outside the window again at the parking lot, getting increasingly anxious with each passing minute. Her food was going stale right in front of her and that didn't seem to bother her, food was the last thing on her mind I suppose. Her inexplicable lack of the immediate surroundings startled both of us when I found myself standing at her table.

"Hi, is everything okay?"

silence

"I don't mean to intrude, but do you need any help? You seem a bit anxious."

"Are you policia?"

"Excuse me"

"Are you a police officer?"

"No, I am not, do you want me to call one?"

She squinted, looking right into mine - judging me. For a moment, it felt like I was standing at the Pearly gates in front of Saint Petronilla herself.

"Have a seat!", she commanded.

I slid into the seat opposite to her, my confused mind begging for an answer whilst shouting curses at me for getting dragged into whatever this was.

"Please excuse me, I have to go use the facilities."

Is she a fugitive? Or has she just committed a crime? Is she a con-artist? Or she has a sick sense of humor and she's just messing with a stranger? I didn't want to accept this, but the worries on her face looked *real*.

She slid back in her seat and took a deep breath. Her eyes locked onto mine and her beauty hit me once again, the seed that was determined to help her - now blooming.

End of part 3

"Can you please help me with something?", she said, with the expressions of a child asking for her mom when she's feeling sick.

Entrapped by her innocence, yet trying to be cautious "What seems to be the problem?"

"I was just walking over to this place and ...." Her voice now just a whisper

"I saw a crime taking place, a guy was being robbed by another with a knife."

"Where did you see this?"

"In the alley right there" and she pointed towards the end of the parking lot.

"There was a mother and daughter getting in their car and I was scared for their life but I didn't know what to do. I was so scared, I just ran away from the scene without doing anything."

"Did he see you - the attacker?"

"No, I don't think so."

"It's okay, it's a good thing that you are alright and that nobody is following you. What I can think of is that you should go to the nearest police station which is like 2 blocks from here and report what you saw to the authorities. There was nothing for you to do at that time."

"But I'm not from here, I don't know how they will react or if they'll blame me for not reporting it earlier."

"You were and are in shock, it's okay just go to the nearest police station and they'll just take your statement and contact information and let you go. You really have nothing to worry about."

I could see her going into the thinking void and before I lost her, I grabbed her hands on the table and looked right into her soul and said,

"You're going to be just fine, you're safe, the reason I'm telling you to go to the police station is to relieve your conscious of this burden and to help the police catch this person. What you saw was horrific but there was nothing you could've done to help at that time."

Out of nowhere, an alternate reality in which she was hurt just hit me like a twisted gift from the bowels of hell.

"I'm so glad that nothing happened to you.", I whispered, my voice breaking; the flood of emotions for this stranger, shocking me.

I could notice her walls of defense coming down, her body language now relaxed, even affectionate and then I realized that it was no longer just me holding her hands.

Stepping back into the reality, I glanced at my watch and said, "I should get going, I have to catch the 7:40 to my friend's place."

"Are you sure I should go? I mean do I have to go?", she whined, was that a look of disappointment? Of hurt?

"Yes, please just remember you're going to be okay. It is scary but they are going to take good care of you."

Wow, is that really all there is to love? Or rather infatuation? Is that all that is needed to make a guy conscious about the very existence of his life? Just a girl with an angelic face and a white dress? God, I was ashamed of myself! Now released from the trance, I got up and left the cafe wondering whether I've just dodged a bullet or lost the love of my life.

But what was that feeling of overwhelming warmness that draped over me when she held my hands, how can the slightest action of someone turning their hands and grabbing onto yours dissipate all the tension in the room, isolate two strangers from the world and put their hearts on the same trajectory?

Walking towards the St. Andrews station, I was lost, lost in my thoughts finding an explanation for the direction my life had just taken; stepping into the 07:35pm train, the answer I had was "divine intervention".

End of part 4

Looking at the cracked ceiling of my bedroom, I couldn't help but wonder how her visit to the police station went. She was so nervous, so scared, I couldn't seem to get the scared look in her eyes and her child-like innocence out of my mind, something about that just pulled at my heartstrings.

Wondering whether I should've gone with her to the station, or stayed there and tried to calm her more by cancelling my dinner plans, I fell asleep feeling selfish.

***

I should really stop going to that cafe, this liquid in the to-go cup from that Mexican food truck is way better than what I had yesterday. Guess it was destiny - me being there at that same time when *she* walked in. I realized that during our brief conversation I didn't ask her name and neither did she; I guess she really was in shock. Witnessing something like what she did can mess with anyone's mind.

I couldn't help but imagine what it would've been like if I had accompanied her to the station; we could've grabbed dinner and gotten to know each other - I would've asked for her name and probably where she was from and where she lived.

What we could've been.

....

Walking hand-in-hand to her place, she whispered "I feel really lucky to have found you that day, what you did for me I knew I was blessed to be there in that moment.", her eyes shyly looking at mine, her head tilted and her steps following the rhythm of mine.

Looking at the way her hair draped over her shoulders, her hand wrapped tightly around mine; I slowed down my pace and held her other hand, both of us now facing each other we embraced in the dim light of the far-away lamp post under a starry sky.

I woke up with a hypnagogic jerk and pulled my mind out of the parallel universe - one which had forked out from the decision that I wish I hadn't made. It was at that moment that I realized that I wasn't going to be the same.

End of part 5

"Hey, hey, Andy, stop. Stop the car man."

"Why are we still moving?", I screamed.

"I don't know just stop it like right now wherever you can", I said pleadingly

I rushed out of the door, slamming it behind me, listening to the now faint curses thrown at me by Andy and rushed to the intersection that we had just crossed. I tap my right thigh just to be sure it's not another dream, I swear I can recognize that hair, that walk, that beautiful vessel in which an angel resides from a mile away after all I was always so close to her and hugged her so many times that I lost count. Even if I was blind, I could still *sense* her aura, *feel* her and *recognize* her before she sees me herself.

Staring at her walking across the sidewalk from me, I assumed that she's going to the police station again as that was the only place worth visiting at that stretch and direction of the sidewalk. Why? Was she in trouble? Did I unintentionally create a problem for her? Did she blame me for it? Is that why I can't sleep at night cause I've been cursed by an angel?

My mind, now in a frenzy, trying to come up with a reasonable explanation for bumping into her like this. By now, I really didn't care. I just wanted to go talk with her, one way or another I have to put a stop to my restless nights even if it meant her shouting curses at me and chasing me down to the station herself - at least I get to walk with her till the station.

I walked briskly to the next intersection and crossed over to her side with me now walking roughly 30 steps ahead of her.

I slowed down my pace so I can bathe in *her* sunshine and then approach her from behind.

I could hear the footsteps catching up to me, somebody sure is in a hurry, all my senses working at optimal capacity.

"What the …….."

She gave a radiant smile and giggled playfully as if she had just tagged me and wanted to say "You're it".

"I'm sorry to have startled you, I saw you crossing that intersection over there and thought I'll come say Hi."

I tapped my right thigh and then my left thigh.

"I'm sorry to have interrupted you. Are you okay?", she said with a neutral expression. What the hell have I done? Do I not like beauty on this planet?

"No, no no, I mean Yes! I'm okay. Sorry. You just surprised me. That's all."

"How are you Miss… I'm sorry I didn't catch your name the last time we met."

"Eden Da Rosa, may I know yours?"

"Adam Dawson ma'am, pleased to meet you."

There's that lovely smile back again. Her eyes now twinkling.

"How did the visit to the police station go that day?"

"You were so right, they were really helpful and it was as you said it would be. They asked me questions and then took my contact number and let me leave. I can't tell you how grateful I am to have met you. It was as if you were put there to be my guardian angel." her eyes searching my face for micro-expressions and I can tell by her face that she liked what she saw.

Guardian angel? Me?

"I'm glad I was able to help you out, to be honest with you I've been thinking about our encounter and how you were doing after witnessing something like that.", I said cautiously.

She gave me a quick but hearty hug and before I could comprehend what was happening, she bounced back and transformed into an innocent child - looking shyly at me, her eyes flashing like stars in the deepest and darkest corners of the galaxy, stealing glances leaving me wondering for the millionth time if this was yet another dream.

"Are you going back to the police station? Is everything alright?", I enquired.

"Yes, I'm just going there to get some documents for my college. As I'm not from here, they need some paperwork from the station, where were you headed?", she replied.

"To the station, just need to run a quick errand. Is it okay if I accompany you there?" My heart was racing, waiting for an answer.

"Sure.", she prompted

We started walking together side-by-side. I admire her courage for dealing with something like this in a totally foreign country, her beauty, her resolve to maintain that purity and innocence even in this messed up world.

"What are you doing later today?", I blurted out.

"Ah, what do you mean?"

"I was hoping we could get some coffee or snacks later in the afternoon."

"I have to go back to my college so I won't be free in the afternoon."

I replied back with a disheartened *Okay*, the severity of which was entirely unintended.

"But, I'm free in the evening if you want to have dinner", she replied and looked up at me – our eyes locked.

"Sure, I'll love that.", I replied hoping to merge the now astray parallel universe.

End of part 6

Sitting in the approximate center of the terrace of this Italian restaurant, dimly lit with medieval lanterns hoisted on either side of the table, I was still admiring her beautiful face. The light from the lanterns dancing on her face hypnotized me, made me forget about the starry sky above, the moon shining right behind her, the sparse crowd around us. Focusing just on her, that's what we both were doing for a while now.

I broke the silence and asked her about her family hoping that a familiar topic would reduce the tension in the air, and calm the storm inside of me.

After a few introductory questions, we started talking about ourselves, what makes us tick, what motivates us. We laughed, cracked jokes when she teasingly said,

"You are a good guy, Mr. Dawson."

"And you are a beautiful soul, Ms. Rosa.", I teased back

At that moment, I sensed that she got nervous. Something started bothering her or at least she was trying real hard to say something.

She took another sip of her red wine, brushed her hair from her shoulder, tucked the other side behind her ear, adjusted her seat, the yellow floral dress complemented her outwardly beauty, as if in anticipation I braced myself for what might come next.

"I want to share something with you, even today when we met near the station I thought about sharing it then cause I didn't know if I would ever meet you again however when we planned this dinner I thought this would be the perfect time to tell you."

Was she being serious or shy I couldn't tell, she was being determined that's for sure, determined with herself about finally saying whatever she wanted to say.

"I know I've simply said that what you did for me in that cafe meant a lot to me. You being there was something… well… normal…. Not the circumstances, those were tragic but I can't help but think that those circumstances ultimately brought you there… there at the table right in front of me……"

She took a deep breath and continued.

"There at the table holding my hand, soothing me with those eyes of yours. I've never felt something like that except with my mom, and making my worries vanish with just your touch and the way you looked at me?"

A silent wind of emotions blew through the terrace of the restaurant, surprisingly affecting only our table. I had to, just had to look away as it was too much, too many emotions rushing all at once.

I saw her hands at the table, *all alone,* her fingers twitching, scratching their counterparts.

I swallowed the emotions of my tongue, eyes and nose and held her hands in mine. I could feel that warmness, the one I was devoid of for so long that I didn't even know existed before I met her, coming over me once again. Her hands holding mine so tightly, yet so carefully not to hurt me.

"I also felt something, something pure yet inexplicable and I couldn't stop thinking about it. I felt so foolish to have left you alone when you needed someone the most.", I replied fortifying my voice.

Looking at the grass below our table, her hands still in mine she let it all out.

"The relief of sharing something like that with you and then to the authorities, you were right, that is something that I needed. I needed time and space to process that tragedy, I know I wasn't at the center of it but somehow I felt that I was *a part* of it, that somehow I contributed to the suffering of that guy, I'm glad no harm came to him but the burden of not feeling safe in your own community, in your own skin that's something no one should go through. It would've been the same for me if I hadn't met you or shared this with you. The way you respected me, my feelings and recognized and appreciated my need for some personal time that touched me. I instantly knew that my friends were wrong, that there are guys in this world that care and most of all, respect having an emotional connection, the guys to whom everything worthy in this world is not just physical or materialistic."

She looked up at me, her teary eyes wandering on my face found their way to mine making them moist.

"And I consider myself lucky and grateful to have been blessed with someone who understands this."

***

Looking at the ceiling I remembered something, I picked up my phone and called Andy to apologize for that insanity. My intentions weren't exactly pure as I didn't really call him just to say sorry. I wanted him to ask me why I reacted the way I did and then guide the conversation to my dinner and then talk about the delightful Eden.

I couldn't control myself and I let it all out. How the first few minutes seemed like eternity, she too was a bit nervous and then how when we started talking, it was never ending like the earth and the sky finally coming together.

We talked about everything - her past and my past, her hobbies and mine, how her family fought tooth and nail to send her here, how she had troubles making friends in her college as everyone thought she's *too nice*, how we connected in such a short time, how we both thought that we are *the one* for each other, and how the restaurant staff had to come tell us that they were closing and we had to leave. I realized that Andy had lost interest but I was going on and on like a stubborn child who's too young to notice the lack of interest from the other person.

But I didn't tell him one thing, one thing that I held close to my heart, one thing that whenever it crosses my mind - leaves a smile on my face.

I had asked her after one of our loud laugh sessions how did you know to trust me in that time and place?

To which she had replied with a shy, timid and sweet smile with her eyes looking down on the table where my hands rested and her hands moving to take those hands - my hands into hers.

"Because of your eyes, your eyes were so genuine, so calm and so deep that I knew I could trust you with anything."

***

All of us have heard and those unfortunate among us (surprisingly almost every girl) has personally experienced the uninvited eyes and comments from those so called *humans* but what I hope that everyone of us understands is this:

That in this world, girls are meant to be beautiful and it is up to us, especially the guys, to admire and cherish that beauty with respect.

JASH WADHWA

"Turning alive the ink on the paper" ~ **Jash Wadhwa (Wolfie)**

An ambivert, deep thinker and wordsmith so it is a given that he and writing are bound to romance. As a young, rational, carefree, and passionate writer, he strives to provide stories that hold real value and provide the readers with something to think and discuss in their minds. When not lost in thoughts, he is in the company of Americano & music, playing cricket, or discussing random theories (pop, science, life, and more), also dedicated and working on his debut novel, 3WAY: Love, Friendship, And Music.

Follow him on Instagram - @amator_insanus

"Can you help me?", Rahul asked yet another person. He joined his hands and submitted his pride. The poor boy from Kasol was a victim to Delhi's crimes. He was about to leave the city, but was it really easy to leave Delhi behind without getting caught up in its traps?

"What do you want?", the man asked in a pissed off tone. For him, Rahul was just another imposter.

"Brother, I am from Kasol. I am new here..."

Before he could even complete, the man cut him off, "I know all this bullshit, 'My wallet is lost. I don't have money to go home.' Trick someone else with that crap not me. Leave me alone, you freak!"

Rahul's hope did not survive the backlash as this was the tenth time he was pushed aside. The ten failed attempts were enough to break his will to keep struggling. He settled on the empty seat beside him. His eyes wet, heart filled with anger, and bleak hopes striving in his mind. The train in front of him was leaving, and his hunger for food and love were haunting him. His train was due in another hour.

'Why Delhi was not the it place for me? I mean, what did I do?' What else could he do apart from self-loathing? Firstly, he was manipulated into believing a hoax promise of a job but he too was to be blamed, as he had trusted someone who he didn't even know properly. Moreover, the previous day his belongings were stolen and when he did seek help from the police, it was in vain. So he had decided to leave the city, without much deliberation. He came to the station, booked a ticket, and while he was on his way to the platform surrounded by the hustling and bustling of the Delhi Central, he had gotten pickpocketed; ticket, money, and even his identity all gone.

"Fuck!", the boy sitting next to him shouted and stood up suddenly, startling him out of his thoughts.

***

'Why hasn't she come yet? She should have listened to me, I would have picked her on time, but no, madam thinks that she is punctual!' I mean, what else can I do apart from complaining!

We had decided to meet here forty-five minutes before the scheduled arrival and now only, half an hour was left! This is Tammana's usual, she will be late, and moreover, she won't even pick up her phone. In such times, you can't even decide whether there's something to worry about or not, because this is how she is, even if her phone is in front of her, it will be on silent and she'll be busy with something else.

Anyways, I was so preoccupied in grumbling and complaining that I completely forgot to share the occasion with you. Tomorrow is our fifth and also the first anniversary. We have been together for five years, and last year on our anniversary, we succeeded in convincing our families. So this year, we are having a trip to celebrate this lucky day. First, we will go to Pathankot, of course, to visit the border, it's my dream. Then, we have a three-day reservation in Dalhousie, from which, on the second day, we will be visiting Khajiar. I am thrilled about the fact that we will be going trekking. After that, we will go to Amritsar; it's her dream to visit the most sacred Gurdwara with her atheist boyfriend.

I was back to ringing her cell again, but the result was same. This is the most irritating thing about her that even if someone will be calling her again and again, she still won't pick, because she doesn't want to listen to the taunts that followed. On top of everything, she even forgets to call back!

Now only twenty-five minutes were left for the train to arrive. 'Relax, she'll come, don't forget that she has the habit of appearing at the last moment too!' I am trying to be calm by reassuring myself. As I have time, I check whether all the things are there with me or not because I have a habit of forgetting things, yes we both are two individuals with irritating habits who deserve each other! Just in case, I don't forget anything, she had prepared this checklist. I am pretty sure that I have packed accordingly, but anyway I have to while away some time so why not. Four pairs of jeans, three T-shirts, three shirts, two nightwear sets, eight underwear, cigarettes, her favourite chocolate, condoms, UNO cards, and a speaker, cool everything is there, check, check, check!

'Ticket! Have I got the ticket?' The question popped into my head and the last memory of the ticket I had was that it was in my drawer. I started checking the side pocket of the bag but it was not there! I was now checking my pockets but not there too. Holy shit! I don't even remember carrying it! But the wallet was still left to check. It was there, neatly folded in my wallet. I took it out for reconfirming the timing and dates. The wallet slipped from my hand but fortunately falls beside me on the bench while I concentrate on the ticket.

'From Delhi to Pathankot, Mr. Luv Shukla, Miss Tammana Singh, train arrival at 1830.' I read and realized that I have lost the track of time. It is 18:10, only twenty minutes left! At that very moment, Tammana called.

"Luv!" She was crying.

"What happened?" I was definitely not getting bright thoughts about this.

"Mom was coming from the market" She paused to sob and then continued, "And she met with an accident! We are in Jeevan hospital. She is in the operation theatre. Please come here fast." She was crying like anything and why won't she.

"Fuck!" I abruptly stand up and grab my bag. I need to get to her soon.

"Luv! I am really scared, her blood was all over the accident scene. I am worried, Luv!" Her voice trembling which helped me in quickening my movements.

"Tammana, please control yourself, mom will be fine, okay! I am on my way and will be there soon. Is dad with you?"

"He has gone to the reception to fill out some forms, Luv, please come fast." She was sobbing uncontrollably.

"Don't worry, Tamanna! I'll be there soon, just be faithful and pray." Usually, it's not that hard to find a taxi here but what is up with the universe today!

"Sorry for ruining the vacation..."

"Are you mad?" There's a taxi "Listen, I'll call you in a minute."

As I end the call, I remember I haven't picked up my wallet from that bench. The taxi had come already, but I had to run back into the station. .

'Fuck, fuck, fuck!' I have completely disappointed myself.

***

"Fuck!", the boy sitting next to him shouted and stood up suddenly, startling him out of his thoughts.

The boy rushed away. Rahul's self-respect got another hit. He was pretty sure that the other boy must have had a good reason for walking away just as he sat down, but the coincidence of Rahul sitting down beside him and the next moment the boy cursing and leaving was something he couldn't shake off. He looked down, and his eyes trailed away towards the forgotten wallet beside him, very subtly he grabbed it like it was his own. He checked for credentials and realized that it belonged to the boy who had hurriedly rushed away.

'Luv Shukla' He read the name. 'I should return it.' This was the first thought that came to his mind. He looked in the direction Luv had rushed, but he was gone.

'Take it for yourself!' his vicious self coaxed him.

'That guy seems to be going through a rough time, Rahul!' the sane one argued.

'So are you! This city has been ungrateful to you since the time you set foot here. Anyone who lives here deserves the same! This is their Karma, their undoing!' the vicious one counter-argued.

'What about your Karma after doing this?' the sane one asked, and Rahul really wanted to listen to him, but the vicious one seemed more practical.

'Stupid! Grab this opportunity in return for all the bad things that happened to you.' Again, the vicious one had provided with a more tempting option.

'You knew that, Sudhansh couldn't be trusted. You had heard that he uses people. Still, you wanted to be a part of this big city, so you let yourself be manipulated by him! You abandoned your family. You ran away from your house! What happened to you was your Karma, not a bad omen!' the sane one said, making him introspect his doings, but Rahul couldn't take it.

'If my family doesn't want to grow, then how is it my fault?' Rahul argued.

'So, how much have you grown this week?' the sane one again tried to persuade him into reflecting upon his choices.

'Do you want me to go back or not?' the vicious one interrupted, he knew this was a trump card to make Rahul accept the bait.

Rahul decided what he wanted and went behind a pillar, diagonal to the bench. He stood facing the pillar, so that nobody could see what he was doing. He took out two thousand rupees and kept them in his pocket.

'This is right, the common ground for both gentleman, I can go home, and Luv will get his wallet back too!' He tried to convince both.

A policeman was seen strutting arrogantly from the direction Luv had run off to, waving his stick.

'You know, he can't be trusted, what if he notices you have taken out some!' the vicious one suggested.

'The other guy had said what happened to me was my Karma, so why don't I give this wallet to this policeman, anyway, it's their job, not mine.' Rahul stated.

'You are really smarter in comparison to that one over there!' the vicious one commented. But Rahul didn't notice, or maybe he didn't care that the sane one had remained silent.

"Officer!", Rahul shouted and rushed towards him, "I was waiting for my train. The guy sitting next to me stood and ran in that direction.", he pointed.

"I am coming from there only, I didn't see anyone. What's the matter?", the policeman asked.

"He forgot his wallet. I guess he was in a state of emergency." Rahul acted innocent. The policeman was pleased.

"My train is about to arrive, and I got to know that it's on the other platform.", he lied.

The officer took the wallet from his hand, "I'll make sure this reaches to its owner, you hurry up, good man, go!" He cheered him.

Rahul turned around and started walking with fast and long steps. He had the plan sorted. He was going to book a ticket, have some snacks, and leave the city with some money in his hands. During his walk, he did look back, at least for a couple of times, to see that the policeman was busy checking the wallet inside out. Rahul had looked back, not to know what the policeman was doing with it, but to check whether he had figured out his lie. After all, when you know you sow the bad seeds, you don't get a good sleep. His adrenaline was so high because both the feelings of happiness and fear coursed through his veins. Lost in his thoughts, he collided with someone and was about to fall but he somehow balanced himself.

"Sorry, brother." He heard a familiar voice, but didn't get enough time to glance at the face. He immediately looked back. It was Luv, he had come back to get his wallet.

Rahul got numb, 'You still have a chance to do some good.' the sane one suggested to him.

'Or else you can sabotage everything and get caught!' the vicious one argued.

"Hey, yellow T-shirt. Wait!", Rahul called out to Luv, but he ignored it.

"I know about your wallet!", Rahul shouted, and Luv stopped and turned. "You must be looking for your wallet. I found it on the bench and gave it to that policeman.", Rahul pointed. He thought he could get away with this.

"Fuck, are you new?! It would've been better if you would have kept it on yourself. My phone number was there on the credentials!", Luv shouted.

Rahul was about to walk away, but shivers ran down his spine and panic started consuming him when Luv held onto his hand.

"Just come with me, it will be helpful. I am amidst of an emergency, please!", Luv begged.

Rahul noticed that the policeman was looking at them and had kept the wallet in his pocket. The policeman was staring at him with big eyes.

"Look, the policeman is turning away!", Rahul lied, and Luv turned to look back. That very moment, he got his hand off from Luv's grip and started running like anything.

Helpless and confused, Luv was frozen for a second, but then rushed to the policeman as getting to the man with his wallet was more logical than running after the witness.

'You know, what's right and wrong, the police forces are all around. You believe it or not, but you know Karma always gives you what you deserve.' The sane one stated while the vicious one remained silent.

Rahul was filled with guilt and fear, his thoughts were haunting him, and he was running blindly, he didn't even look back for once, just running like it's the end of his life.

'People who believe in karma can't be at peace after doing something like this, it is due to their belief that whether right or wrong, justified or not, their actions will come back to haunt them!' On the other hand, what do you think? Did Luv get back his wallet? And if he did, did it have all the money? Did Rahul get caught? If not, then what did Karma have for him ahead?!'

CHANDANI BHATIA

"So many thoughts left unheard, So many words left unwritten. Now is the time to hear my ink speak." ~ Chandani Bhatia

A Supermom with a super power to weave an ordinary string of words into heartfelt musings! Writer to awe-inspiring poetry that leaves you wanting more of each and every word or emotion expressed. Winner to many poetry events and Author to a few anthologies, she is an inspiration to all. Although a teacher by profession, her passion and skill dwell in the writing field.

Follow her on Instagram - @simran_speaks_writes__

Yet another day where Richell was anxiously waiting for Ranjan, who had departed the house a night before and his arrival, an uncertain instance. With his mobile phone switched off, there was a wave of panic that hit Richell time and again. Into the silent night, her phone blared indicating an unknown number calling her. The next words were just a blur for Richell as she couldn't recover from the shock of the three words that were reiterated to her on the call. After about an hour or two, there was a knock on the door. Still dazed, she gathered herself to answer the door and the reality hit hard when she sighted an ambulance and a couple of ward boys carrying a white sheathed motionless corpse. It was Ranjan's body. After the paramedics had tried to relentlessly revive him back, he was declared dead and heart attack was the cause for the untimely demise. This came as a shock to Richell, as there had been no past medical history or explanation that could be derived to justify his death. The commotion caused, invited the neighbours to crowd around, some of them consoling the newly widowed bride, others just perplexed by the situation. Immediately, one of the well-wishers called up Austin, a very close friend of Ranjan and Richell's informing him of the incident. Aghast by the call, Austin hurriedly informed their families and started the arrangements for the funeral. In the blink of an eye, everything came to an end for Richell. She stood lifeless, with no tears to shed over the death of her husband. But why wasn't she crying?!

Let's rewind back a little!

College, this is where their story started. A new transfer student, quite the eye-catcher amongst his batchmates, fell desperately in love with a girl, with awe-inspiring dreams and a strong headed personality. Ranjan, being a late transfer, got Austin, his batchmate to prep him up for the finals. What he didn't know was that the girl that troubled his thoughts, was Austin's best friend. To his surprise, one day even Richell agreed to help him catch up on missed work and soon he got to know about Austin and Richell's friendship. Later on, the three became inseparable due to their tight-knit bond of friendship. Even though, both Austin and Richell knew that the Dean was Ranjan's dad, they never shunned him or even sucked up to him, which made Ranjan really happy. Soon after, Ranjan proposed to Richell after a lot of deliberation and she too said yes, as she felt the same about Ranjan.

Time flew as their relationship blossomed and then the time came for the exams. With the exams and everything, Richell dived deep into her books, that she didn't find time to meet up with Ranjan or even Austin. As soon as the exams were done, the results were out in a day. The arrival of the results came as an unabated shock. As always, Richell had undoubtedly secured the first position but Ranjan, on the other hand, had failed in three subjects and had merely border lined in the other two. Dismayed by Ranjan's lack of interest and preparation, she cut off all ties with him and refrained from talking to him. Lost in her thoughts of Ranjan, she had forgotten about her own career, her dreams. Austin had been observing this dishevelled state and had grown anxious because he couldn't see the girl he loved, Richell, fighting battles with herself. He had attempted a lot of times to make it known to Richell about his feelings but had failed in doing so. With graduation around the corner, he suggested to her on getting a job so that she was distracted from the present circumstances. Even after that, whenever she'd hang out with Austin, she couldn't help herself from mentioning Ranjan. The only solution to this, according to Austin, was that he talked to the man himself personally.

Barely surviving all the tough circumstances in his life, Ranjan had delved into a state where he adopted ill ways to while away his time. Drugs and cigarettes had replaced Richell and Austin in his life, leaving only regrets and anger to consume his mind. On seeing this, Austin refrained from speaking to Ranjan, keeping his insanity in mind and thought that it would be convalescent to speak to Ranjan's parents about the present situation. On hearing, Ranjan's parents were appalled and treatment was the only option that sufficed the current situation. They had to work out ways in order to get Ranjan back to his normal without him coming to know. Gradually, Ranjan was coming back to his sane self and things were starting to get clear to him. Consumed by nothing but regrets, he was ashamed of himself and didn't have an ounce of courage to face Austin and Richell. Surprisingly, Austin made up his mind to meet up Ranjan after he heard about his progress which frankly left Ranjan gobsmacked and anxious that after a long time, his friend wanted to catch up with him.

Café Bistro, their hangout place in college, was the venue set for the reunion of the two friends. Both of them were equally apprehensive about the meet and didn't know what the future entailed for the both of them. At first, it was quite awkward between them but once Ranjan led the conversation by apologising for his actions, things became amenable. Things started to become coherent to Austin when he came to know that Ranjan fell into bad company due to which he had changed over the numbered days.

"So, what are the plans now? How have you decided to change the course of your life?", Austin asked. After a lot of thought, Ranjan replied, "I am yet to decide but I feel I have lost this battle." Austin couldn't let him lose hope because after all, he cared a lot about Ranjan but more so about Richell, who he knew would have encouraged Ranjan to move forward. "How can you say that, Ranjan? You have a life ahead of you, push yourself to move on!", Austin told Ranjan. "Trust is a very fragile thing, and I was successful in breaking that. Who would believe me now? I have nothing left!", Ranjan sadly stated. "You have everything, Ranjan. Your family, Me and even Richell!", Austin frustratingly responded. Hearing Richell's name, his eyes shone with delight and surprise. "Even Richell, after all this while?", Ranjan exclaimed. Austin, simply nodded with a small smile on his face, as he knew that Richell's name was enough to push Ranjan out of his helpless zone. "First thing, I am going to do is take my exams again, get a decent job and then court her.", Ranjan said after a lot of pondering. On hearing this, Austin was happy only on the outside and had masked his true emotions which were swirling from within. He suppressed his own happiness for Richell because nothing else mattered anymore.

Things were starting to fall into place for Ranjan with a good percentage in college and a great job. Time also flew by in an instant within these two years. It was time to reunite with his lady love and prove to her that he was a changed man. Ranjan fished through his wallet for Richell's number, which Austin had given him but hesitated several times, unaware of the repercussions. Anyways, he fought up a lot of courage and dialled her number. After a few rings, the connection was made. Ranjan was very tensed due to which he had become numb and couldn't utter a word, on the other hand, Richell was just frustrated to hear no responses to her hello. As soon as she was going to cut the call, she heard a hello which definitely caught her undivided attention. Did she actually hear Ranjan's voice or has she been thinking too much about him?! "Hey Richell, Ranjan here! Remember?", Ranjan asked sheepishly. "Wow, hi. I never thought that you'd call me. Where did you get my number from, by the way?", Richell enquired, utterly confused by the turn of events. "It doesn't matter, Richell. What matters is I am sorry for disappointing you and hurting you but I am a changed man now. I have a decent job with my exams in the clear with distinction written on my certificate. I have everything, except for you in my life. It's all because of you, that I am able to cope with life positively. I don't know what'd I do without you.", Ranjan rambled on and on, leaving Richell teary-eyed. "Richell, please say something. I am getting tensed here with you quiet, I am just losing my mind. Will you marry me?", Ranjan cried out in the stressed state. "Oh, Ranjan! I don't know what to say. Yes, of course but you won't revert back to your old ways, right?", responded Richell, quite an emotional mess. "When you are there, I just won't be able to! Oh God, you have made me the happiest man alive right now.", exclaimed Ranjan. After talking for awhile and catching up on all the lost times, they cut the call. Ranjan felt on top of the world at the moment, he had achieved his dream – Richell whereas Richell, over the time, started to have feelings for Austin but she never expressed to Austin her inner turmoil.

But the call with Ranjan, her first love had resurfaced and that was a trump card over her feelings for Austin.

In the meantime, Ranjan planned to propose Richell in the most exquisite manner possible and to treat her well. He planned out the entire date and called her to tell her to meet him at the park, the one where they had their first date. He arranged a picnic style date with fairy lights hanging from the trees and red plaid picnic mat with brown basket full of goodies. Ranjan glanced at the arrangement and felt excited but the weight in his pant pocket was enough to make him nervous. Just at that moment, he saw Richell get down from the cab, looking around for him. He immediately realised that his surprise would get ruined if he didn't rush over. "Richell!", Ranjan shouted, jogging towards her. Richell couldn't believe her first love was standing in front of her and he still had that boyish charm which made her fall in love with him. Ranjan, with her consent, blindfolded her and guided her to their spot. As soon as he removed the blindfold, Richell gasped with surprise at what lay in front of her. When she turned around, she saw Ranjan on his knee, with a box which held the most beautiful and delicate ring she'd ever seen. "Marry Me!", Ranjan asked, with nervousness laced voice, still unsure whether his lady love will accept his proposal. Richell, emotional by all of this, couldn't utter a yes so simply nodded excitedly and tears gave way when Ranjan slid the ring on her finger. After an excited chit chat, mushy moments between them and stolen glances, they left to inform their families. On hearing, their families were overjoyed and left no time in prepping for the wedding rituals. From the engagement to the wedding, everything was a blur and the two souls were bonded in a nuptial manner. Everyone was ecstatic about the couple except for Austin, who still couldn't get over his feelings for Richell but he kept a happier front so that no one would be suspicious. Honeymoon was the next plan on their itinerary and as expected, it was a 2 week filled with complete bliss for the couple.

On returning back, they were shocked to hear that Ranjan's father was transferred to another city because he had sexually harassed a student. Furthermore, they even discovered that this is definitely not the first time this was reported. His transfer forced both Ranjan's parents to move to a different city, leaving the newly weds all by themselves. A number of truths of Ranjan's past was unveiled to Richell and shock would be an understatement of what she was feeling. Ranjan reassured her by informing her of the medication he was currently on and he felt better than before which lessened the stress and tension she was undergoing. With all the truths out, the newly weds could start over fresh and support each other through thick and thin. Things were moving forward smoothly until the day Richell fell severely ill. Although, it was a mere fever which required medication and lots of rest as advised by the doctor, there was no major improvement in Richell's condition. Things went downhill after the deterioration in Richell's health and the midnight mishaps, where Richell was found screaming in aggression. Doctor after doctor was changed but no one could explain the bizarre behaviour of his wife, making Ranjan extremely worried and tensed about the current scenario.

On hearing the predicament in the newly weds' life, Austin decided to visit Ranjan and Richell. Ranjan was grateful to see Austin at his front door and thought that maybe a change of visitors would bring an improvement in his beloved's behaviour. Despite seeing her best friend, there was no change in Richell's aggressive behaviour which made Austin suspicious of her condition. After keenly observing Richell, Austin talked to Ranjan and told him that the possible cause of the situation may be paranormal. Hearing this, Ranjan was appalled as he was not a person who believed in spirits or ghosts or exorcism so he thought that Austin had completely lost his mind for even suggesting that. The next few days gave Ranjan some time to ponder over Austin's prognosis because of the occurrence of multiple incidents confirming his suspicions. The crisis at hand had become terribly worse when Richell tried to kill Ranjan and that was the last straw for Ranjan's patience. The only person who could help him with the speedy recovery of his wife was the person who was somehow right about his opinion. Austin, on the other hand, was surprised to see Ranjan with a change of mind. They both got to work on contacting the local priests and exorcists who could help them get their Richell back. After a lot of calls and frustrated talking, they hit jackpot with a Babaji who lived 4 hours away from their place and was willing to look into the matter. The very next day, both of them left for the 4 hour journey, with hope within that things will go back to the way it had been. On reaching there, Ranjan was quite hesitant to meet the Babaji because of the spooky, eerie surroundings but Austin reassured him that this is their only chance to bring back the Richell they once knew. A mysterious, meditative man with an unusually long beard was seen sitting on a solitary stone with his eyes closed, droning out 'Om' time and again. Stealthily, Austin and Ranjan moved towards Babaji, looking around to absorb the sights around them.

"Kya samasya hai, bacche? (What is the problem, children?)", asked Babaji, his voice booming across the room. Both of them got startled and immediately hurried in front of Babaji, who beckoned them to sit down. Gradually, Ranjan opened up about his situation, divulging all the details to Babaji, necessary for him to make the right call. After a lot of contemplation, Babaji chanted some mantras and told Ranjan to perform some bizarre rituals on a new moon night. Ranjan and Austin, after making sure that they have everything, left for home to execute their plan. A week left for the new moon day and Ranjan was tensed as hell because his heart still denied to accept something as a spirit to have possessed his wife. But seeing a slight change in Richell's health and behaviour, he started to trust the superstitious beliefs reiterated to him by Austin and Babaji and knew that what he was about to do will definitely work.

The day arrived and Ranjan's nervousness had shot through the roof, as he had started second-guessing everything. Just as Richell crossed his mind, he gathered the courage and left home just an hour before the clock struck midnight to reach his destination – the graveyard. On reaching the graveyard, he started setting up for the ritual, when suddenly he felt the hairs on his nape stand up and a chill ran down his spine. Recalling all the warnings told by Babaji, he just quickened his movements and ignored the eerie presence behind him. "Ranjan!", called out the voice behind him, awfully similar to Richell's, luring him to turn around. Fearfully, he turned around and panicked to see no one there. With his heart pounding within, he once gave a look-over at his surroundings and turned around to see a women draped in white saree, standing very still. Looking at this, he got very scared. The woman suddenly charged towards him and frightened out of his wits, instead of running away, he just dropped dead at that very instant.

Cut to the present, the funeral with all the rituals were performed, with all the relatives and friends consoling Richell and Ranjan's parents. Ranjan's mother was howling very loudly, unable to stop the shedding of tears, as she had lost her one and only son. Ranjan's father too was unable to speak, still shocked of what had happened. The only person who didn't shed a tear since the time Ranjan was pronounced dead was Richell. Everyone thought that she was traumatized by her husband's death and she was void of any emotion at all. Austin kept staring at Richell to read what was going through her mind but couldn't get through her because she was a closed book today. Heart attack was the cause for Ranjan's death but what led up to it was still unexplainable to the people there, who knew his medical history. Gradually, everyone left after the ceremony except for Austin, as he had many questions troubling him to which he needed the answers now.

"At last, I got my revenge! This one is for you, Di. You got the justice you deserve.", Richell exclaimed. "What do you mean by revenge? Murdering Ranjan was your plan?! What is going on, Richell?", enquired Austin, baffled by Richell's statements and shocked to hear that the plan all along was Ranjan's death. Richell said, with a smile gracing her face, "Thank you Austin, I couldn't have done it without your help. Anyways, do you remember, the time Ranjan transferred to our college?!" Austin nodded and replied, "Oh yes, I distinctly remember. His dad was the new dean of our college, but I remember thinking that his appointment was a bit last minute."

"Yes, it was last minute, because my dear father-in-law has a track record of sexually assaulting female students of his college for entertainment purposes. He had been transferred to our college, due to this very reason. The girl, who was a victim to this heinous crime of his, was my elder sister. She was in her final year and she needed the Dean's recommendation for one of her jobs. On requesting a recommendation letter, she was blackmailed into doing something she didn't want to do and as she struggled for her life, he brutally took away every part of her. Her death shattered my family forever and it's never been the same since then. Fortunately, Ranjan's family didn't know I had a sister or else, getting my vengeance would have been difficult. Knowing that Ranjan was their only child, I knew that Ranjan's loss would definitely scar them forever and that is what they deserve. From pretending to love him to behaving aggressively, everything took a lot of effort but at the end of the day, it all turned out to be successful. Thank you Austin for sticking by my side till the end even though I kept you in the dark for a very long time. Now, my sister's soul can rest in peace and my entire family can finally get closure since the time Di died.", Richell told Austin, getting teary-eyed thinking about her beloved sister.

The turmoil within her heart and mind had finally come to an end and she could live peacefully knowing that justice had been achieved.

DR. MANSI SINGH

"Wear your battle scars fearlessly just like your sexuality transparently with pride!" ~ **Dr. Mansi Singh**

An Empath who lets her poems convey the emotions and the stories to tell tales of their own. Always wants to jump out of her comfort zone and experiment with genres, especially those which can cause quite a controversy. A happy-go-lucky person who believes that 'whatever you get in life is what you have the courage to ask for'.

Follow her on Instagram - @monlupe1996

"What matters most is how well you walk through the fire"
- Charles Bukowski

Nick has walked through hellfire for the past 5 years. It would be sugarcoating it if it is not mentioned how miserable and gut wrenching his life had become as of lately, a 25 year old beautiful man, yeah beautiful, because his elegance cannot be compared to anyone else, anyways, Nick met Rafe the love of his life in Arizona during his graduation period and they fell in heads over heels for each other until Rafe's father, the most feared mafia and current leader of Archwery family got to know of his son's personal affairs. Salvatore Archwery was not someone to be crossed so Rafe feared for the life of his lover and ultimately, broke the everlasting promise of love and shattered Nicholas Bane. Grief stricken Nick moved back to Italy to live with his family and to complete his education so that he can take over Bane's enterprises. That was just the beginning of his misery.

NICK'S POV

The air around me was getting stale and suffocating, that with every breath, I was inhaling I was feeling as if it's my last puff of cold air. What more can I do to stop this suffering? In that moment, I thought it was a good idea to live inside my car for a few days before I reach there in this cold weather. Looking at this stolen Sierra, I can only comprehend what had gone wrong with my life or is it true that I am paying for my sins and will burn in hell for who I am and what have I become. While tenderly touching Aiden's golden tuft, all I can recall wholly of my former life is the prayer I recited every minute for the past 5 years.

"All I can feel is sorry,
I am so sorry for myself.
Why living on is such a hell?
God, why did you make me like this,
So abnormal,
So full of sins.
Every day, it's killing me to live on,
Is loving someone that great of a sin?
I can't help but fall in love with him,
Even if he never wanted me for a minute.
I pray on with all my might,
With all of my last breathing self to spare my son,
Please spare him and let him love someone who will
love him back."

***

With the prayer, I recalled the jarring memory of my former life. Yeah former, because I won't go back there ever, well not alive if Beth's goons find me before I have reached Arizona. With Beth's name came the agonizing memories, she had given me.

***

"Are you a good for nothing, bastard? Why in the hell did I marry someone like you? I told you to stay away from my room at all times, Can't you see that I had company at that time?", Beth shouted angrily, with her vein on the forehead popping out, indicating the level of her anger.

(With harsh words followed the merciless beating)

"Beth, I would not seek you at midnight if Aiden was not so hungry. Please feed him for the sake of God.", he said, with desperation glazed tone.

"What the hell is wrong with you? You want me to feed that brat. Just buzz off before I kill your miserable self and find some servant to feed him. Charlie, throw him out but do not forget to reward him very well for wasting my time.", Beth said while spitting on his face. The reward was none other than a round of lashes and beatings.

"What are you even saying? Beth, he is our son and it's our responsibility to feed him, not some servant." He was terrified of the repercussions of talking back to Beth but his son's well being was his first priority.

"Listen, you lowlife and listen very carefully. You are here to just produce an heir for Ricosta family and take care of him but remember, don't you dare turn my blood gay too like your nasty self.", Beth said while pointing a finger at him.

***

That was our last conversation before she threatened to kill me because her brother was talking to me and she thought I was seducing her little brother. The beating that came after that was one of the most painful ones of all.

Aiden never deserved a cold-hearted Dona as her mother but when she slapped the 4-year-old Aiden right across his cheeks, I was so vivid with fury that I pushed Beth back to stop her abuse but fate played out very differently. She fell to the floor and twisted her ankle. On seeing her twisted ankle, she started to howl very loudly, alerting her goons, after which they had a field day beating me black and blue. But as soon as I recovered, I limped my way inside the closet which was more of a home than the rest part of the house and took out the emergency bag that I had been saving for my escape for a very long time. But the most difficult part was taking my son with me. Taking Aiden with me meant I would be carrying the heir of Ricosta family, which is extremely dangerous but leaving my son here meant throwing him into the sea of crime and blood.

And here I am, planning my next move to remain undetected till I reach Arizona but the snow, last night, had put my initial plan on the back burner. With little to eat and piles of snow in front of me, I can't seem to think of anything right now. Should I call for his help? Will he pick up my call after what has transpired between us in the past? But he is the only one who can save me from dying right now, even if he denies me, he will most definitely save Aiden. Without any hesitation, I took out my cell phone and started calling the only saved contact number in my phone.

The ringing from the other side was really making my heart go all crazy, how many years has it been?

***

"Rafe? Why did you call me here?", I asked him with surprise in my voice because we usually meet at lunch time.

"Nick, listen we can't go on like this, this is abnormal and totally frowned upon by everyone. I don't have a future with someone like you.", Rafe replied while throwing a hard glare towards me.

"What? But Rafe, you said we will go somewhere else away from your family to live together and marry someday and eventually

adopt some kids. That was all a lie to you", I said, even when my voice was breaking with sheer agony as if I was living my worst nightmare.

"You want me to run away from my destiny?! I am the next leader of Archwery family and you can never be my Dona. I can't be gay like you, it was just curiosity that lead me to propose to you.", Rafe said, each word with pure venom dripping from his voice and stabbing my heart.

***

I can still hear his words echoing at the back of my mind.

Rafe – Hello!

I was shocked to hear the roughness in his voice but still, I could recognize his voice anywhere even if it was hardened with years of darkness that he may have seen.

Rafe – Who the hell is this?

Nick – Rafe!

All I could hear is paper stifling and a booming "get out now" from the other side. He was yet to say a word to me.

Rafe- Nick! Nick, is that you?

Am I dreaming or is that really concern I can hear in his voice?!

Nick – Yeah, Rafe, it's me, Nicholas.

Rafe – Where have you been? I was searching for you for so long.

I didn't expect to hear that from Rafe, of all people to say those words. Why was he searching for me?

Nick – Why? Why were you searching for me? To kill my gay self so that I don't infect anyone else? Don't worry your wish came true because I was ever so miserable that anyone can get in their lifetime.

Rafe – Nick, what happened? Where are you?

Nick – Rafe, save me please, I can't take it anymore.

Hearing his voice, had broken something in me yet again, the dam that was closed for so long was overflowing with pain and anguish now and I was full-on sobbing as if I was back in his arms again. For these past years, I was living for Aiden and the company dad had built for me. But truly, I was numb and devoid of any emotion until now.

Rafe – Nick, I will reach you within half an hour, just hold on tight, my love. I will take you out of there and please stop crying and tell me what happened? Where were you for the past 5 years?

Nick – Rafe, after we graduated, I moved to Italy and joined Dad's company and completed my masters there in the Alps. In the last year of college, I met Beth Ricosta. She was my friend or so I thought. She discovered that I was gay and got me drunk, after which she raped me. I was unconscious but in the morning, she told me she wanted some weak and rich guy to be her leader so that she can be the Dona of Ricosta family and lead them without anyone hindering her actions and provide them with an heir so that they won't question her leadership. I refused to obey her

and they killed dad in front of me, they didn't even spare mom, Rafe. She locked me in my own company until Aiden was born. After Aiden's birth, she gave me a closet-sized room to live with Aiden. You won't believe it but my son looks just like me. So I took the beatings and abuse till now for Aiden's sake but one day, she hit Aiden. Rafe, I was not strong willed to tolerate that so I pushed her and her goons beat me to pulp and left me there to die. But after regaining consciousness, I ran away from Montana with Aiden in a stolen car. For the past week, we are trying to reach Arizona.

Rafe – Your son, Aiden, he is with you right now? Are you truly alright, my love?

Nick – Yeah, Aiden is sleeping because we were running since the past week and he was really tired after not sleeping properly.

Rafe – Just 5 more minutes, Nick. Hold on tightly, I got you.

Nick – Thank you, Rafe.

The call got disconnected. How will he react when Aiden will call him his papa? Will he be disgusted with me that I told my son that he has two fathers, one is his dada and other is his papa who he will meet someday. Well, I will deal with that bullet when the time will come eventually for now I will rest. But why am I feeling so weak? Oh, well starvation will do that to anyone. With droopy eyes, I adoringly watched my son's angelic face before closing my eyes.

***

RAFE'S POV-

NICK NICK NICK

That was the only thing going on in my mind while I navigated through these busy roads. It's been years since I had driven myself somewhere especially for someone but still this was Nick, we are talking about. I could make out the shadows of my people following me closely as they know that it's about Nick. Yeah, my whole goddamn empire knows about Nick because they were there with me, searching for him for the past 5 years.

But how the hell did Ricosta's leech get her hands on my Nick? Well, I will ask her when I will slit her throat. Every single member of their empire will pay for those 5 years they kept Nick with them. I really made a grave mistake by walking away to save Nick's life from dad that day. I humiliated and degraded my one true soul mate because I was not strong enough to fight back. But after dad passed away, I got the precedence over all the decisions of the clan because I was their leader then and my sole purpose was to bring Nick back into my life. Therefore, the search began 5 years ago and was in vain but destiny wanted us together.

While thinking such thoughts, I noticed a beaten-up Sierra, stuck in piles of 2-foot snow and I could faintly make out a figurehead lying on the steering wheels of the car. That must be Nick's stolen car he mentioned. Stepping outside I could feel the cold seeping inside my trench coat but determination to see Nick, won over any physical barriers.

When I opened the car door, I was pushed back in a spiral of my own memories. 7 years back when we last saw each other, his pain-filled teary eyes looked back at me with both anguish and betrayal I had caused him. He never begged me nor stopped me but I knew then and there, I broke something in him that day. But now, I am looking at the aged face of my only lover, beaten and bruised and yet his mass of golden spun hair gave him the look of an angel that had been in a war for too long. As compared to myself, he is and always has been a beauty and I am like a dark version of him with steel-grey eyes and a mob of dark midnight black hair. As I took a closer look, I could make out the hard muscles underneath the jacket and another mass of golden hair sticking out from Nick's jacket.

Big, bright blue eyes were looking at me like I was an alien. As a matter of fact, he was actually the replica of my lover and not an ounce of Beth could be seen in him and I was grateful for that.

Aiden – "Papa!"

Our son was surely super cute, Nick, just like you and he is so tiny and trying to wake Nick up but why was Nick sleeping for so long.

Rafe – "Come here little one. We will wake your papa together, okay?!"

Aiden – "Papa, Dada hurt. They hurt Dada. Dada saved Aiden from the bad lady"

What is this little one saying? Was he calling me Papa and the bad lady must be Beth then I suppose. Nick had told his little boy that I am his Papa, maybe I still had a chance to have my Nick back and maybe I don't need to resort to begging on my knees so that Nick will take me back. But that b***h will die a miserable death for laying a hand on my family. No kid should see their dad get beaten up by some crazy psychopath.

****

Archwery Clan POV

Every member of the Archwery clan kept their distance and watched their leader with both loyalty and respect. They had seen Andrew Rafe Archwery search for his lover for the last 5 years when they lost track of Nicholas Bane in Italy and faced the worst possible wrath of their leader. They knew that their loyalty will fall upon their Dona because Nicolas Bane was there Dona in their hearts. Everyone was shocked to see a little boy in their leader's arms which was an exact replica of Nicholas Bane. Their leader was shouting for the clan Doctor to take a look at the Dona.

****

Doctor – "Leader Dona is unconscious due to dehydration and low blood sugar. I can see bruising in the upper abdominal region so there is a possibility of broken ribs and swelling in the left ankle region too. We have to start him on proper IV and monitor him overnight."

Rafe – "Do whatever it takes for you to make him better and Ron, arrange an emergency meeting regarding the demolishment of Ricosta clan by tonight. I want your Dona to open his eyes without looking back at his past."

Ron – "Yes Leader!"

Aiden – "Papa!"

Rafe – "Yeah, little one? Are you hurt?"

Everyone was shocked to hear soft and tender words coming out of the most powerful and feared mafia leader's mouth.

Aiden – "Aiden hungry, Papa."

RAFE POV

Aiden's stomach was growling and I was enraged after seeing and hearing Nick's battered condition. On top of that, Nick was unconscious because he must have starved for the past week to feed the little one all the food they had but our child was still hungry as hell. I will only be satisfied after butchering every single one of them, the Ricostas.

Rafe – "Zander, Ryan, we will be heading to the nearest food court. Alert everyone and take care of your Dona with your life. I will catch up with you all in half an hour."

Zander – "Will do that brother. See you at home."

Spending time with this little munchkin is everything to me right now and taking care of his Dada my only priority. We headed to the nearest pizza junction and I helped Aiden to stuff his face with the good yummy stuff as he liked to call it. Half an hour later, I reached the Archwery mansion and commanded everyone to start the meeting with the other clans in an hour.

Aiden – "Dada! Aiden wants Dada!"

I stepped into my chamber and took Aiden to my lover's bedside where he was sleeping ever so peacefully.

Rafe – "We have to let Dada sleep okay, Aiden."

Aiden – "But I wanna sleep with Dada and Papa!"

Rafe – "Okay, little one come here. Let's not disturb Dada much."

After Aiden slept, I decided to complete my next task and that was to destroy the Ricostas. Deep down to my very core, I was aware that Nick won't be happy that I killed people but this was something necessary for my peace of mind and to sate the blood lust, I had been feeling. Every clan leader and their most trusted ones were present before me and looked at me with both respect and fear.

Rafe – "Your Dona is finally with us, my brothers and sisters and I want the Ricosta Clan to not see the next light. Inflict as much pain you can on them as they did on your Dona. Slaughter them. Butcher every single one of them. Torture them and then kill them off. Have I made myself clear?"

Everyone – "Yes, Leader!"

They will do as I say because I rule above them all and now with my Dona and my heir at my side, I will rule without any obstacle. But the most difficult task will be to persuade Nick to rule by my side. Well that is a battle for another day.

***

AUTHOR NOTE

Set in the backdrop of Israel (god contends), this piece of writing deals with an issue which is significant yet not a preferable dining table conversation around the globe, which is, homosexuality. Though it has been declared legal in most parts of the world, it still causes a glitch in the throat while discussing about queerness. It makes people feel as a misfit in the society as in the case of Nicholas Bane and there are people like Andrew Rafe, who just to prove their masculinity disregard their sexuality by suppressing their real emotions and then end up messing their own as well as other people's lives. The climax of this story is a proof in itself.

The question is, is it really necessary for us to prove something or to feel a 'fit' in some place at the cost of our own happiness? We are in the second decade of 21st century, we (humans) have done wonders in every sphere of the world but when it comes to the little delights of life, we compromise.

Fairy tales are more than true:

Not because

They tell us that dragons exist,

But because they tell us

That dragons can be beaten.

ANWESHAA DEB

"Writing in an exam hall is a pain but such a good medium through which people can speak out even if it's on paper. The day I realised it's strength, there was nothing stopping me from going on to express myself with words and phrases dipped in pen and ink." ~ Anweshaa Deb

A Biophysicist with a great vehemence for writing and getting her readers transfixed in her words. Being a crime thriller buff, she doesn't refrain from adding every inch of buzz and anticipation. She has released her music album 'Brishty Obelay' on Youtube.

Follow her on Instagram - @inca_r_nation

"Marvellous!", exclaimed Sheila, standing on a rock in front of Jogini falls, also considered a shakti peeth (symbol of women empowerment). To her left was the gurgling stream eager to join river Beas and in front of her, were the giant mountain peaks clad in Emerald and Pearl. Sheila, a second year student of Presidency University in the Department of Life Sciences studying lifelessly only to get a job one day and follow all her passions. Although she was an extremely bright student but I believed that she could have been the best in anything due to her sheer intelligence and talent.

I am Raktim, a student of Jadavpur University, a passionate photographer and an extensive trekker with a very rare certificate of appreciation for rock climbing. My mother, being a typical Bengali woman was over possessive and shouted 'BABU' so loudly as if only she had one. On one such occasion, Sheila suddenly turned around hearing an echo of 'BABUUU..BABU..BABU..' from the hill tops of Green valley in Shimla because my Mom not seeing me thought I would exploit my rock climbing skills and go down the steep valley in order to present some heroic act.

"All mothers are tensed, Beta. You'll understand only when you yourself will be a father" Again a very common statement by Bengali parents. The words came from behind me just when I was about to take it out on my Mom.

Mrs Sohini Mukherjee, Sheila's mother, also a renowned lawyer defended my mom followed by Mr. Monomoy Mukherjee and my father Mr. Asit Ghosh. It is believed that Bengalis outside West Bengal get along very well and this was not an exception. Right from the very next day, we were having lunch together, booking an SUV for Manali and not to mention, I was undeniably the happiest person in the group.

19th October 2018

It was almost 2:30 in the afternoon when we were passing through Mandi, a place somewhere in between Shimla and Manali. Overcrowded cacophonous roads and markets were something I had least expected in a hill station. People seemed to be unexpectedly busy although it would have been a very usual sight in Bengal because it was the day of Bijoya Dashami.

"What's the matter?", Sheila asked our driver Sunil. To which he replied that in Himachal, it is a different sentiment altogether dated back to the 16th Century AD when Raja Jagat Singh was the king of Kullu.

On hearing, about a peasant named Durgadatta possessing beautiful pearls, he gave a cruel order of killing Durgadatta, on refusal to give the pearls to the king. The King never understood that those were pearls of wisdom and Durgadatta, knowing his plight submitted himself to the fire, cursing the king.

"Whenever you eat, your rice will appear as worms, and water will appear as blood"

The king, in search of solace was advised by a Brahmin to bring a deity of Raghunath from Ayodhya which was done without delay and established as the ruling deity of Kullu. So we learnt that today was the day when Raghunath is taken out on a Rath throughout the city and Mandi, being close to the place, also celebrated this day. As we approached towards Kullu, there was an increase in both crowd and commotion and we came to know that every year, 4 to 5 lakh tourists come here. Sheila was listening to every detail very attentively and also noting down in her writing pad which made me think whether she will be the next Byomkesh Bakshi or Mitin Mashi.

"Jaldi Chalo... Yahan se hat jao (Hurry up...... Move away from here)" A few men were shouting while banging the car window. I was able to sense a sudden change in the mood from celebration to chaos and calamity. People were yelling and running and unmounting their deity from the palanquin and the closed cars were told to move out fast. Sunil informed us that all the deities followed by individual clans meet at the famous Dhalpur Maidan of Kullu, the main attraction being the deity of Raghunath. After about 5 minutes of journey at about 10 km/hour, we sensed that things were quite out of control. Sunil had a 'terribly tiny' conversation with one of them and completely broke down to tears adding to our nervousness. Shocked as hell, he could only tell us "Raghunath is no more...." Sheila immediately checked the news in Google and it was the headline of every news channel. People were using a few extra vocal chords to let people know and feel, how grave the loss was while others were busy in the blame game. Aunty and Mom were trying to catch a glimpse of the deities but Sheila in the meantime, tried gathering more information from Sunil and the crowd running past us. Finally, we reached Manali and found our cottage was near Hadimba Temple, although a little off centre but had a beautiful panoramic view of the lush green mountains followed by snow clad ones.

"Hi", I initiated seeing Sheila in the next balcony who responded with a warm greeting followed by the entry of her father, a nature lover and also a self proclaimed landscape photographer.

"Hello, Young man. Oh! You have a nice camera... may we head for a photo walk in a while?" I was overjoyed with the proposal and accepted immediately.

Mall road, Manali – a place worthy of all praise and hype was crowded with people otherwise happy and gay, except for today's mishap. A rooftop cafe made us lucky enough to capture the crowd mood as a whole. Beauty of Manali was so mesmerizing that we forgot today's tragedy for a while. Although, I doubt Sheila had forgotten anything and was surely trying to gather information. After having Baked Trout fish and Mutton Momo with a mug of hot coffee, Kaku and I came back to our den only after taking a few photographs of Hadimba temple on our way back.

"Babu, we were ordering coffee and pakoda. Do you want to have?" My answer was obviously negative. I locked myself in my room until I studied all the photographs and had picked the best ones for my final folder.

"May I come in?", asked Sheila and entered almost simultaneously.

"May I see the pictures that you have taken? Actually, the ones captured by Dad are not very clear." After her second statement, I couldn't stop laughing which made her smile shyly for the first time, since we met.

"Are these all that you have captured?", asked Sheila.

"Obviously not, I showed you the best ones" I wanted to tell but instead I just told "Oh no no... These are just the few that I have segregated till now."

Sheila was seeing each and every photograph way more minutely than any judge of any competition I participated ever. Her face turned quite different from the shy smiling face a few minutes before.

"Where did you take all the pictures?", asked Sheila

"Few in Hadimba temple and the rest on Mall Road...", I replied briskly.

"And how much time did it take to reach Hadimba temple from Mall road?

"Umm... it was 30 minutes of walking plus 5 minutes of your Dad's smoking.", I replied only to get back a frown in return on which, I again couldn't help but smile.

20th October 2018

It was 8:30 a.m. I realised that Dad was already awake, quite restless and speaking to someone over the phone.

"I have to leave right now. Something very urgent has come up... SP Kullu was found to be dead today in the early morning.", Dad informed us and hurriedly got ready.

Mom was extremely upset because she made Dad promise that this would be all vacation and no work. My Dad, by the way, is DGP Asit Ghosh posted presently in West Bengal. Sheila, Kakima and Kaku came to our room to ask for breakfast and were also upset on hearing today's incident but not more than Sheila because she missed the opportunity to get a close view of the incident. Sheila was hell bent on visiting Kullu maidan where the event was arranged and Sunil also agreed to take us while the others decided to take an Auto Rickshaw to Mall Road.

"Baba, can you please keep a lookout for a group containing two Negroes and few Chinese men in Mall road? We will have to inform uncle once he comes.", Kaku responded with thumbs up to Sheila's request.

We headed towards Dhalpur Maidan. It was my first trip with Sheila and I was thrilled. Sheila was also thrilled but I guess only to be a part of the investigation, perhaps her first one. On arrival, we found it to be a no entry zone although it was not like we did not expect it.

"What are you both doing here?", asked my dad, only when I was about to call him.

"Dad, she is really interested in this case since yesterday. She has some passion in this field and now that you are involved, we wanted to grab this opportunity. Please Baba allow us and we also have something to show you regarding this once we reach hotel." My pleadings didn't go in vain and we were in.

We were taken to the crime spot by Dad. Just because I have seen all the detectives go for ground searching, I too went for one although in vain because it was trespassed by thousands of people already. Dad was busy talking to fellow officers from investigation agencies. I looked around to find Sheila was missing as she was searching the perimeter of Maidan of which I was clueless because apparently the crime scene was where I stood.

"Uncle, do you have any information regarding any cross border drug racket operating here?", asked Sheila.

"Yes... actually here there are quite a few drug rackets but sometimes we are awkwardly helpless that we cannot arrest them. Why do you suspect that?" Dad avoided a few obvious words.

"Uncle, I found these and it is very unlikely that people coming here to pay respect to their deities will carry such smoking ingredients in their pocket." Sheila handed over a few cigarettes to Dad.

Dad and I were quite surprised to see that she found these even after a thorough checking done by the department although Dad seemed to be a bit more shocked, the reason for which I failed to understand.

"But these can be of any hippie or visitor... How can we link this to a drug racket?", I asked .

"Yes, it could have belonged to anyone but it is not... It is surely a clue..." Dad left me more confused.

On our way back, we stopped at SP Digvijay Singh's place where his wife and daughter were still in shock while her husband's body was sent for post-mortem. We went inside for a while because Sheila wanted to see his bungalow and after a brief chat, we headed back to the hotel while Dad stayed over there. Immediately after we got down from the car, Sheila held my hand and ran towards the hotel door which obviously was a bit awkward for me.

"What happened?", I asked after reaching the reception.

"We are being followed, Raktim." She sounded tensed but something ran down my throat to my stomach, hearing my name for the very first time from her mouth.

"Babu, where were you roaming the whole day? Do you want to eat something?" Mom, Kaku and Kakima were all in our room having a chat over Coffee, Pakoda and Momos.

I joined them at once because I was a hungry Hippo by then, totally exhausted but Sheila seemed to be busy with her phone and my laptop seeing the photos over and over again.

"Baba, did you notice the kind of group I mentioned today?", asked Sheila looking at the pictures and taking a bite of the steaming Momos.

"No dear. Although I asked in almost all the cafes about such a group but no one could tell anything.", Kaku replied very innocently.

Sheila with a horrified expression, yelled at him, "Baba! Who told you to ask anyone?"

"But I just tried to....", Mr. Mukherjee, baffled by her daughter's behaviour, stopped giving any explanation.

By that time, I was looking at her and she gave back a meaningful look. We were convinced that our direction was indeed taking us closer to the truth, and danger. We kept quiet to avoid any further panic and changed the topic.

"Stay safe Babu... and keep the doors closed... I am on my way home..." Dad's text came. Sheila must have already informed him that we were being followed.

Later in the evening, I tried to see the pictures from the other day but my mind constantly shifted to the window and men who were following us. I wanted to discuss with Sheila what would be our next step but that would have been awkward because she was with her family in the next room.

Next I could hear a sound of a car entering the driveway followed by a couple of bullet shots and then a few rounds of firing. We rushed to the driveway and Mom was shocked to see that Dad's right hand was bleeding although not because of bullet but a piece of glass that was probably broken by repeated firing. Dad rushed to us and told us to get back to our rooms immediately.

"Why do you take such risks all the time?" Mom was extremely tensed and so was Dad in fear of Mom's scolding.

"I am fine... They already went behind the boys and will be caught soon.", Dad reassured everyone.

"Thanks beta... you have really helped us in searching the Maidan. She is an extremely sharp child I must say..." Dad was nothing but all praise for her while both of us looked at each other.

"Digvijay's post-mortem report has already arrived. Six bullets have been used... We have to check with today's bullets if it matches."

"It means either the goons are still novice therefore used six of them to be sure or this was a hatred murder... although first one is more likely in this case.", Sheila came up spontaneously and Dad was again impressed by her deduction.

"Uncle, I told Dad about an unusual group containing two/ three Chinese people and few Negroes which I noticed while going through the photographs captured by Raktim the other day." Although it was Sheila's version, according to me it was scanning the photographs.

"But Dad actually asked all the cafes in Mall Road about them from where I am afraid, they were alerted." Although, Sheila seemed guilty of what happened, Dad was smiling.

"So this is apparently the reason why they didn't leave till now because they had to get us first otherwise they would have already left. So I assume the deity is still in the town. Hello.. Shekhar, give orders of closing all the exit points from Manali and nearby towns. Also, deploy a search team for a group containing Chinese and Black Boys."

"Thanks Mr. Mukherjee... You might have just helped us in getting our deity back." Kaku was totally confused by Dad's statement because a few minutes ago, he got a scolding from his daughter for the same reason.

Meanwhile, the constables came back and informed that by the time they reached Hadimba temple, the boys were gone although they went all the way down to the Mall road.

"I think they went for Old Manali because Sunil told us that road to the left from Ghatotkach Temple leads to Old Manali. I came to this place twice before so I know..." Dad was already shocked to hear this which was only increased by my second statement.

"Dad, I'm thinking of something else... that is even more serious... I am quite sure there is a trekking route from Old

Manali to Solang Valey...or Oh Shit! Dad, they can even cross the border through Kaza." I was all horrified.

"But they can't trek for so long at this hour of the day. So shall we go for Old Manali right now, Raktim?" Dad was not convinced with Sheila accompanying us

But I took the chance and told, "Oh yes, you may come. I'll be there."

I had a hunch that they will be staying somewhere near the Manu temple because the trek route starts from there.

"Dad, they are in Hikerzzz Bundle. Lets search there because the owner also has a cafe in Mall road where Kaku must have asked for them."

"Beta, both of you stay here", Dad instructed us and went for a raid.

Suddenly, we heard a few firing sounds after which everything went silent. The officers came along with the group of boys followed by my Dad carrying the Deity of Raghunath. Unbelievable as it was, we were clueless as to how to react.

"Is this true? Is this possible?" I looked at Sheila and she was equally clueless.

"Inspector Thakur, send this asap for a forensic test", ordered Dad. We understood that even Dad was unable to believe his luck that he was presently holding the ruling deity of Himachal.

"Uncle, something else must have been happening while Raghunath was only used to distract us" Dad looked puzzled but couldn't deny because everything was seeming quite obvious.

"Sir, please contact Home Minister's office and tell him to immediately increase the border security. Something very serious is going to happen especially towards the North Eastern part." Dad disconnected the call and told us to go back to the hotel.

21ˢᵗ Otober 2018:

In the morning news paper, we came across the horrifying news that 62 Quintals of Charas (*Cannabis sativa*) and a few bags of Heroin ampoules were recovered from an army base camp near Gulaba (place not disclosed).

It was almost 1pm when Dad came back and we were quite eager to know the details but Mom was more interested in his well being though. Finally we came to know the details which apparently go this way that Raghunath's deity being guarded by army personnel could have gone missing only with their help. Sheila handed over a few cigarettes same as those that were found by my Dad in SP Digvijay Singh's pocket. This created two possibilities :

- He also found them in Maidan just like Sheila but then the question arises why he wouldn't pick all of them up.

- He was also given those cigarettes by the same person who was also connected to the Deity disaster.

"If the second option is being considered then why was he killed?", asked Sheila

That was a real question whose answer was given much later. "Dad, how did you know where the drugs were hidden?" Here came the importance of the cigarettes which were of a Chinese brand and not very common here. So it must have come from across the border and involvement of army was already discussed.

"Dad, how did you get to know which military bases to look for?"

"This was something that we got to know by interrogating the group of boys from Old Manali"

"But the credit behind searching army base camps in Gulaba and Solang goes to you Babu. Only because you told there was a trek route... Interrogation of the boys let us know that a consignment was scheduled yesterday and the other one already arrived.", replied Dad

Army already being on alert informed that two large sacs were seen in the bunker of which one contained Charas and the other one was filled with injection ampoules, initially thought to be Heroin.

"Yes Uncle, that is published in the newspaper too. Isn't it true?" Dad looking at Sheila, replied, "It's actually much more dangerous but if published, it would have caused unnecessary panic. The bottles were marked as heptavalent antitoxin... a drug used to treat Botulinum neurotoxin affected people."

Shocked and speechless, we were eagerly waiting for him to complete.

"By that time I received a call from the forensic lab where I had already sent the cigarette samples from both Maidan and Digvijay's pocket. It revealed something nasty that the cigarettes were actually baby milk powder containing Botulinum spore that causes a severe Botulinism amongst the infants and babies."

"That's how I assumed Digvijay Singh's son was dead. Am I right Uncle? Actually I have seen his son in their family picture and I couldn't see him when we went to their house. I mean it's quite unlikely to keep such a small kid away from his mother and sister when such a disaster occurred." Sheila's statement surprised and pleased Dad so much so, that he patted on her head twice. The kind of appreciation I hardly got!

"Yes, his son somehow got hold of the poison while playing in the house and was found to be seriously sick after a day or two. He survived for another 5 days before..... His father guilty of his son's death decided to accept all his misdeeds and expose the racket. This is apparently the reason of his death..." Dad somehow managed to narrate the story without choking.

"Where did you find the toxin Dad?"

"It was just a decision well-made based on a hunch. Stacking of so much Baby food would need some considerable amount of space which could not be kept in an army camp. Therefore we thought of trying a temple very near to the camp which could have been a probable storage site. By luck, it was proved right." It seemed Dad felt the relief of saving so many children all over again while narrating the whole plot.

22nd October 2020

We were off to Vashisht Temple although our initial destination was Gulaba view point but Mom didn't want to go to such a place ever in her life. Obviously, no one was in their merriest mood and mostly the topic of discussion was how cruel our society had turned. Sunil thanked my Dad multiple times for saving lives of so many children and Raghunath their protector.

"Sheila, promise me that you will try for IPS or IB. You have a strong gut feeling and a natural talent of keen observation." Dad patted Sheila with a pride.

"Dad at least you have someone to bank upon." I knew that Dad always dreamt of me being an IPS officer.

"Will you all go for a trek to Jogini Falls?", I asked addressing everyone.

"No beta, we had just enough of adventure in these three days."

"But I want to go Babaa... Pleaseee..." I hoped Sheila got the permission.

"Ok but come back early... and Raktim, see that she doesn't try to do something impossible."

I was more than happy to take her for a trek in fact our first date.

"Do you go for trek regularly? I mean you were very keen to come for this." My words left her a bit embarrassed.

"No, actually I never went for one.", she replied softly.

It took me a few moments to assume that even she wanted to spend some time with me. Rest of the journey was completed quietly except for a few casual chit chat.

"There... there... Just a few more steps...", I assured her, in case she was feeling tired.

Reaching Jogini falls took five more minutes and for the first time, I had seen her so lively, one with the nature, running all over the place like a child.

"Can you take me there Raktim?" Although I remembered her mother's warning but I couldn't disappoint her.

At the top of the peak, came the sound of a roaring water fall and a shrill scream, "Marvellous.... I Love You... Manali..."

GAGAN ULUVARU

"To put out the voices in my mind and to help people through their journey in life's path!" ~ **Gagan Uluvaru**

Not-your-usual Engineering student, who adds an emphatic flair to the world of writing, creates gripping plotlines that will keep you hooked on for long and fortes in the art of contemporary literature. A reader as well as a writer, both which are equally ardent passions of his, he is a fanboy to the K-Pop world and is forever an Otaku.

Follow him on Instagram - @_clear_shade_

It is that time of May where you see a moody weather in the town of Burford. It has been cloudy and rainy since the mid April. Buford is a small town with happy people all around. Medieval architecture is the beauty of the town. Thundering clouds, fast breezing wind, people rushing to get their work done and go back home was the current status of the town because of the weather.

Daniel, a 27 year old city man, recently moved down here from London after taking a long break from his job as a software developer. He needed a new and peaceful start after his girlfriend Clara decided to visit the graves permanently. Life had never been easy on him since college. His only happiness was taken away from him and thus, after months of agony he decided on a new start and to find a new meaning to the life he lost.

As days rolled, Daniel found a routine in his new home town and also found a decent job as a web developer. The life he had now was normal, a job that let him work whenever he wants, wherever he wants and a peaceful town with lots of things to look around at. His favourite place is **The Priory**, a restaurant and also a bed and breakfast dine. It was a British fare served in a charming, 17th-century building with a garden patio & five guest rooms. It had a huge glass window which spanned almost the whole front end of the restaurant with tables outside for dining, the interior of the place was mainly wood & charming decor. The whole restaurant gave you the real British vibe in it. They served, **the best coffee in town,** or so he says. That was his constant place in the evenings. A hot coffee in the rainy weather, a window seat, a beautiful view and a beautiful book in his hand. That was what you call a perfect life. Daniel was happy with what he was doing, but there was a part of him still missing and he desperately wanted that part of him back.

Days changed to weeks, and weeks to months. It didn't take him long to get settled into the town's buzz. There were people he was familiar with by now and as expected his best buddy, Fernando Torres was the owner of The Priory. Torres or Torry so addressed by his close friends, was a 65 year old man who immigrated to Burford with his parents at a very young age. Torry and Daniel had become good friends ever since they had a chat over a cup of coffee at the corner of the restaurant every evening. Torry knew exactly how to make his customers feel at home and also knew what his customers always wanted.

Daniel lived in a leased house on Priory Ln. His days were monotonous, getting up early morning and going for a walk. Music kept him company all the time during the brisk morning walk. After returning back home, a cup of coffee is something he can't miss, then breakfast later on. During the day, he would work on his projects, do other chores and also cook lunch after which a little nap to make the day. He would wake up around four and head to The Priory, have a nice chat with his mate there, later he would read a book or scroll through his phone. If not for these activities, then he'd just look out the window with his headphones on and some music he liked. The rainy weather wasn't going easy on the crowd. He loved it. Every bit of the surroundings felt as if it's tuned for him.

***

1 year ago

It was 8 in the morning, Daniel had just woken up and Clara was still asleep. A ray of sunlight came through the tiny pores between the curtains and fell on Clara's face. Daniel just admired her watching her beautiful face, running his hands through her hair and the thoughts of how lucky he was to find a girl like her, kept running through his mind. She was his only constant in this fast pacing life which he'd found hard to adjust, she was his strength and light. His thoughts were interrupted by her movement.

"Good Morning, little princess. How was the sleep?", Daniel smiled and asked her. "Good morning, love and it was great.", she replied as she wrapped herself around him resting her head on his chest. "We have to get up at some point of the day, you know that right?", He said with a laugh. "Nooo, let's just sleep the whole day. No wait. Let's just lay down here forever", she said and hugged him even tighter. Such a child, she was. This childish behaviour was what pulled Daniel more towards the cave she carved for him and that was why he used to call her 'Little Princess'. In the end, he always gave in. That was exactly why they were in bed for a few more hours.

***

Couple of months had gone by and the days were clear now, as a matter of fact Daniel's mind and body was clear too, he had even stopped taking his medications since he thought it wasn't relevant anymore. It was like he was setting the weather for the town or the other way around. This coincidence kind of intrigued him sometimes and he would laugh at his foolishness when he thought that it may be true. His time for a better life was on it's way he thought.

It was one of those great evenings where the sun setting made the sky look like an art work, the few birds flying in a flock at a distance look serene and the hustle-bustle of the streets gave a very homely feeling. As always, Daniel was by the corner reading The Nightmare by Lars Kepler. He was too deep in the book when the bell hanging from the door, rung. A girl walked in and sat down at a table which was at the opposite end from where Daniel was sitting. She was a normal town girl with the most beautiful green eyes which looked like gems as sunlight fell on them and she had black long luscious hair. She was from out of town, anyone would comment on one look at her. Nobody here knew who she was, not even Torry; she sat there in the corner looking out with her earphones in with a frown. A waiter took her order for a coffee and a couple of cookies, Torry saw the frown on her face and thought of having a talk with her. Torry, as always with a smile on his face and a cheerful mood made great conversation with her, but it didn't take long for her to say she needed some space. Torry respectfully got back to his work.

Daniel got up packed his book inside the backpack and started walking out, "See you tomorrow, Torry", he shouted. "You too, Dan, my man.", shouted Torry from the counter. While heading out, Daniel noticed the girl in the corner table who was sipping the coffee extremely slowly and he paused for a couple of seconds because nobody could really ignore a pretty face such as hers. He came to his senses and then continued to walk back home which was a few minutes away. On the way, he thought about the girl with the green eyes and the raven hair who he knew from somewhere but he couldn't put his finger on it. Evening turned into night and at his work table too, he couldn't concentrate, just merely thinking about the girl with the green eyes. He thought 'That's a beautiful girl' and his heart started beating a little faster while he pictured her face. He had a genuine smile on his face, that smile you get when you know everything is great is life. Thinking about that beautiful face, he went to bed.

It was evening and nothing had changed much but Daniel wanted to see that girl again. He sat in his usual place, wishing she would walk in and oh, she did. She too sat in the same table as yesterday and ordered the same thing. Like Daniel, she was a routine follower. Today, instead of diving into the book, Daniel sat there observing the girl. She just sipped hot coffee, nibbled on some cookies and looked out the window, listening to whatever music she was into. He was lost in her when Torry walked in on him. "How's it going, Dan?", Torry asked, startling Daniel. Sheepishly, he replied, "Nothing much the usual, I have a project to finish tonight so I'll get going now" and then he left the place. The girl was excessively on his mind now, her eyes, her face, the way her hands moved to adjust her smooth black hair, he just couldn't stop thinking about it. It was like falling in love all over again but this time, it was with someone who he barely knew, he didn't know her name, where she was from, how she came into town, what she does for a living, nothing, zilch. And the most scary part was he didn't want her to get involved in his life because of what happened to Clara. Clara's death had broken him to the core and he felt responsible for what happened to her. With all these thoughts in his head, he fell asleep in the cold room.

***

6 Months ago

*It was a normal day in the lives of Daniel and Clara, the happiest couple in the city, as they told with the fall out laughter leading that, they were indeed the happiest ones. In the evening, they both had coffee at their usual café with a pretty normal conversation to accompany. It was 5:30 pm then and Daniel had to leave for work as it was his night shift. They bid good-byes as Daniel left for work. Clara was on her way back to their apartment, skipping & singing on the street like a little girl, she was a joyful soul. ".....**I'm thinking 'bout how people fall in love in mysterious ways, Maybe it's all part of a plan**..." Ed Sheeran's song playing loud in her ears, when all of a sudden a car from the other side, swerved across the street destroying everything in its path, slams into her.*

There was carnage everywhere, panicked people running around, crying, shouting, it was a mayhem. Clara was unconscious and was bleeding like a river. The ambulance arrived after a while and she was operated on as soon as she got to the hospital. On hearing the news, Daniel rushed to the hospital as his whole world was crashing down on him. He reached there to hear from the doctors who were still operating. He could barely see her, all he could see were doctors and the equipments they were busy using. Clara was fighting for her life, she was fighting to get back to him. But it's wasn't enough. At this point, she couldn't hold on. Her blood pressure dropped and her heart stopped beating, she had coded out on the table. As the doctor came out and informed him the time of death, Daniel's mind went blank. He had gone numb. There was nothing left in him now. It was like an end for him, he just sat there processing what was told to him. Not moving an inch nor shedding a single tear thinking "Only if she didn't drop me off"

***

Now evenings for Daniel was only about observing the girl with the green eyes. Just observing her from far away. Days passed then weeks and now it was a month since he fell in love with this girl, this green-eyed stranger who was still very much a stranger to him as he was to her. One day, like all other ones she didn't show up at the restaurant which made Daniel first think that she may have some other place to be then thoughts started to run wild and soon, he was worried over his mind. He ran out to search all around the town, she was no were to be found.

With a tensed mind he came back to The Priory's to take back his book that he had left in a hurry. He noticed a blue Post-It inside the book *"You thought only you could observe me from far? I did my own research. Just wanted to see your reaction if I wasn't there for a day, good to know someone cares about a lost soul like me. See you tomorrow... You know the place & time... - Nameless soul"*.

First he felt the weight drop from his heart and mind as he read this, then he giggled on his own stupidity. Now that he knew she also knows about him, he was way too excited. He said goodbye to Torry and went back home. He could sleep that night because the next day he was going to meet her finally. But although he was in love with her, he didn't know her opinion. He felt stupid for some unknown reason. The next day was a good day as he was done with all his daily chores before he set out to The Priory for his evening coffee. Today, it was special because he was not going to be alone in that corner table, it'll not be just him today. He got in and thought "Where should I sit? In my usual place or hers? I think hers would be good cause she'll be comfortable there... No, wait I think it should be mine because I'll not be comfortable in hers and I am way too nervous now" going back and forth he stood there near the door when someone whispered in his ears "Are we gonna sit or just stand here blocking the way?".

For an instant, he was startled before both of them broke down into laughter, finally coming to an agreement to sit in the middle. "So what's the name of the Nameless Soul?", Daniel asked with a smile. "It says nameless for a reason and one should not ask that", she giggled. "If it is forbidden to tell your name then what about where you come from? On that note, where are you from?" "Hey, you ask a lot of questions for a person who you just met. And yeah, I am not supposed to say my name, place or anything else. If you are okay with that, we may continue our conversation", she said playfully. Their conversation went on for a couple of hours, neither knew each others names or anything personal of any matter. After that, they left to go their separate ways. This became the new routine for the both of them. They both became great friends in a few weeks time. Even now, both didn't know anything about one another other than their common interest and what's trending which felt oddly strange for Daniel but he was fine with it as long as she was.

***

Both were looking into each other's eyes lost in their own world, it was Clara in his arms. The world seemed so beautiful that instant. The park was dancing to their mood. Not long after, the sky turned dark and the clouds gathered all around with a black hue. Wind was rushing all over the place carrying dead leaves and twigs with it. He looked around and felt a sense of chill in his hands, he looked down to see Clara's soulless body in his arms, her green eyes staring back at him and the long black hair drenched with blood.... Scared beyond anything, Daniel woke up from his sleep, he was sweating like he had just run a sprint. He sat there with all these negative thoughts in his mind. Eventually, he did fall asleep.

***

He woke up in the morning and went for a walk. The weather was a little cloudy, unusually for a summer day. Piano recital was buzzing in his ears and the thought of last night's nightmare still haunted him, all the signs making it worst like this morning's weather. Back at home, he sat at the table with fried eggs, a couple of toasts and a glass of Mango juice. Today, he didn't follow his usual routine, didn't complete any of the work he was scheduled to do and his head was a mess. He thought he would talk it out as much as he could with the girl in the evening. Like every other evening, he went to The Priory on time, the weather had gotten worse. Dark clouds, rushing winds, no birds flying around and no sun to be burning bright. He sat at their table and waited for her. Torry saw his friend Dan worried and came along to sit down, he waited for Dan to talk and when he didn't, Torry initiated, "What's going on, brother? What's bothering you? Scared of the weather? It happens every year now and then, so don't be gloomy, she'll be here soon. Cheer up!" Saying that, he left Daniel to his own haunting and unnerving thoughts. He knew Dan wouldn't say anything if he didn't want to and if he wanted to, he wouldn't need to ask, all he would have to do is sit there till he talked. He waited and waited for many hours. But she never showed up, Daniel waited till The Priory's closing time but she didn't show up.

Now there was no sleep coming to him for all he could think about was Clara, the restaurant girl, his nightmare and also the weather. It was driving him crazy. The next day he waited the whole day in The Priory's but she never showed up, the day after that and the days after. By this time, Daniel had lost his mind and Torry was worried about Dan. Like a god's worse sense of humour again, his mood matched the weather, his struggle to make sense of all these factors drove him more crazy but all he could do was wait and that's what he did. He waited for her every evening, every day watching the sun set and the birds flying far away. The girl with the green eyes never really came back.

ELAKKIYA SRUTHI

"The ink in my pen shall provoke any soul to think, introspect and speculate. I write to express and inspire!" ~ **Elakkiya Sruthi**

Quite an avid writer of quotes, poems and short stories which range from the romance genre to exploring the inspirational side of things also. 25 short stories and counting with over 50 poems, are part of her achievements with a novel in the making. She has been a co-author as well as a compiler to many anthologies. Her plotlines have never disappointed her readers so be prepared!

Follow her on Instagram - @i_pen_my_mind

Tring Tring!

Tring Tring!

The cell phone placed on the chaotic desk, kept blaring and vibrating continuously indicating an incoming call. Jack turned his head in the direction of the ringing and on checking the caller's name, he was pleasantly surprised to see it was Jessy Evangiline, his college sweetheart. As soon as he accepted the call, Jessy squealed through the phone, "Hey, Babe!" "Hey Sweetheart!", Jack chuckled to hear her enthusiasm but was mildly curious to know what had gotten her spirits up. "Babe! Are you free in the evening?", Jesse questioned him, mentally hoping that he is free. "Yes, of course! But for what exactly? Any occasion?", Jack probed, wanting to know more. She meekly replied, "My parents are travelling out of town and they'll return by tomorrow. The good thing is I will be alone. Will you be with me till their return?" Jack was thrilled at the fact that he could spend time with Jessy even after his hectic schedule. "Wow, that sounds great. I will be there by 7 pm.", he exclaimed. They both disconnected the call after reiterating their love for one another.

Crime rates had started to climb up and being an officer in the forensic department, he had been piled up by an indefinite bundle of criminal cases. Currently, he was exhausted by the consignments that kept stacking up on his desk. The only thing he looked forward to in his entire day was talking to Jessy. Jessy was the love of his life, who had become his number one priority since college days. First impression of the couple left people in awe of how perfect they were together. Even though, they both pursued Bachelors in

Forensic Science, Jessy went on to become a writer as she had no interest whatsoever in criminal investigations. But without her parents' compulsion, she would have never met Jack and their love story wouldn't have kick-started.

As promised, Jack left office by 6:30 pm in order for him to reach Jessy's house by 7 pm. Once he neared her house, his heartbeat had elevated just thinking about Jessy. He parked his bike behind her house and climbed the tree that led to the balcony of her room. He entered her room to find it empty, much to his astonishment. Overwhelmed by excitement, he yelled out "Jessy" every now and then. But his enthusiastic yells was met by an eerie silence. He thought that maybe she was playing with him but after searching the entire house, he was thwarted. Where was she?! The resounding ringing of the door-bell broke his reverie of thoughts and he walked stealthily to the door. Looking through the peephole, he was baffled to see her parents standing there, who were expected to return tomorrow. He did not waste time in exiting her home, unnoticed because his presence in the house would have raised quite the alarms. No call, no message! What was going on?! The white rose that he had brought for her, had wilted away due to the intense clenching of his hands in frustration and dismay. Throughout his journey back home, he couldn't stop reflecting about Jessy's whereabouts.

***

Two days had gone by in a jiffy but Jessy was still missing and no clue led up to her disappearance. Jack was getting impatient by the minute, just thinking of all possible outcomes but nothing was adding up. He got to know that her parents had filed a complaint with the police. Knowing that she was the only child of her parents, he knew what they must be going through. Both of them were having a hard time coming to terms with the fact that their beloved daughter had gone astray mysteriously. Her mother was mourning incessantly without food and rest while her father kept staring at one of her many photo frames. He dearly missed his daughter but he had to be strong for his wife, who had taken this even worse than him. Somehow, he persuaded his wife to eat food so that she didn't fall sick. While nibbling on small bites, she constantly muttered, "Where will she be? Did she have her dinner? What she will be doing? We shouldn't have left home in the first place. This is our mistake. Jessy, please return home!" By the time, she was done with her string of words, she was on the verge of tears.

Here, Jack was going insane just assuming the worst and so he decided to handle the case by himself, knowing that the police would fail to find her. He knew he alone wouldn't be able to crack this case so confided his matter to Jeeva, one of his closest friends. They both sat down to plan out where they were going to start this hunt and how they were going to proceed. They did a stake-out near Jessy's home, keenly observing her parents and their whereabouts. As soon as they left home, both of them broke into the house through the balcony of Jessy's room. They went around looking for fingerprints and unusual clues that could lessen the intensity of the mystery. But when they failed terribly in finding something, they understood that it may have been a planned kidnap or maybe it didn't happen in the house. But they didn't want to leave any stone unturned so they resorted to using the UV light for finding fluid prints about and around the house. They did come across a very significant clue, dried vomit in the garden whose sample they collected for testing purposes. Every fluid print they collected was sent for a test and the results came out as an unabated shock. Surprisingly, the DNA in the vomit sample didn't match any other known DNA, collected from the house. With this result, they concluded that a person from out of this town, had something to do with Jessy's disappearance. They knew that with such negligible amount of information, they were far from closing the case. After droning over the case day and night, Jeeva thought it was wise for Jack to step down and take rest. "Take a break, pal! You are tired and sulky, which is definitely not helping you in this case. We will find her, you hear me?! Pop a sleeping pill and sleep at least for tonight.", he advised Jack, hoping his friend follows through on his words. On the back of his mind, he reluctantly had agreed to Jeeva's advice because he knew that if he did not take rest, he would become eccentric in this hunt for Jessy.

Next morning, Jack's mobile blared loudly in the voice of his queen and he immediately attended the call. It was Jeeva, who had called to check up on him and was updating him about the matters at hand. Once he disconnected, he had just remembered something very important but now that was lost in the space of his mind. Again, his phone started blaring indicating Jeeva's call and then it clicked. A year before, when they both had bought the new model of Iphone, they had decided to record each other on their mobiles. Soon, that had become the ringtone for the both of them and using that, he could find out the location of his queen, thanks to Siri. The constant ringing and vibrations transported him back to the land of reality and he at once answered the call. He excitedly revealed the plan to Jeeva, who then decided to be there at Jack's house within 10 minutes. Once they traced her location, they set off on the long journey, for the very first time hope bloomed in their hearts. Within an hour, they were nearing their destination but the strange thing was that it was the starting point of a forest. Jeeva whispered under his breath, "We are near, just 300 kms more." According to their plan, they called up their friends to help out as a search party in this dense and strange forest. A total of 60 people had assembled, even though it was quite dangerous to tread into the forest, only because people adored Jessy a lot and that made Jack overcome with emotion.

Jack devised a fail proof plan and according to that, everyone was supposed to start from the peripherals of the forest and gradually move towards the center of the forest. Drones and many types of gizmos were put to use in order to track everyone's location in this impenetrable forest and once everything was set into place, the search began. They walked for quite a while, taking no breaks in between but she was nowhere to be found. Jack ruffling through the densely covered forest, came across a stand-alone white rose. He kneeled before it and at that very second, he felt a weird sensation but he couldn't shake off that feeling. He called Jeeva and once Jeeva answered, he broke down, "Jeeva, I feel something is off. She is here, I can feel her presence." Jeeva reassured that they will surely find her and that he needs to be strong for the both of them. While he was speaking to Jeeva, Jack was getting a notification of a second call from one of the people in the search party. The person said that he just detected a human presence in this forest other than them. Jack told him to find out more about this person without getting caught in the process and to stay right there. Right after that, Jeeva called him and told, "Jack, you need to get here. I am interrogating a man who lives here. Maybe we can get a clue out of him of where Jessy is." "Wait a min, Jeeva. One of the people from our group had also called to tell me the same. I will be right over.", Jack responded.

Jack didn't waste any further time to rush to the young man's house and was curious to know what the young man had to say. Jeeva was sitting opposite to the strange man who was actually smirking at him as if he was awaiting Jack's arrival. "Who are you? Where are you from? What do you know?", Jack enquired, cutting to the chase as time was running out. "Why'd hurry? What will you take – tea, coffee, water?", the queer man responded. He was quite young and maybe the same age as Jack but that didn't matter because this man was infuriating Jack. "Excuse Me! We are..", Jack was cut off by the man who completed his sentence for him, "….looking for a girl. Yeah, I know!" Both Jeeva and Jack were baffled as they had not disclosed this information to the stranger yet. They glanced at one another and then send questioning glances at the man, who was smirking quite arrogantly at them. Jack broke the awkward silence by asking, "How do you know?" At this, the stranger laughed haughtily and replied, "Wow, Jack! I never expected you to forget me. I had been waiting for you for the past two days but you are no good a forensic officer, people peg you to be. Remember, someone by the name Oliver?!" Jack racked his brains and his eyes widened when everything started to make sense to him. He was enraged and before he could say something, Oliver spoke up, "It seems you remember everything. Yes, I never interfered or hijacked your relationship because I was planning something big. Three years and here we are! I knew you would do everything in your power to get her back. I was eagerly awaiting your arrival for the past two days." "Cut to the chase, Oliver!", Jack growled with fury at the audacity of this guy. "Calm down, Jack! Shouldn't you have met her by now?", Oliver questioned, the smug look on his face triggered Jack's anger to intensify. But they were both confused as they didn't meet Jessy on their way to Oliver's house. Was he playing with their mind?! "The white rose! Ring any bells?!", Oliver answered their doubts.

Hearing this, Jack went berserk and charged towards Oliver to punch him mercilessly but before he could do anything, Jeeva confronted him and made him realize that Jessy was important. Without giving Oliver a second glance, they rushed out of the house and frantically hurried to Jack's prior location. The white rose stood, unwithered in its place and was blooming very beautifully. Jeeva shouted, "Everyone dig into the ground. Hurry up!" Even in the chaos, the rose stood unaffected, thriving within the minute. Oliver's words were ringing in Jeeva's ears and he thought to dig under the white rose. Sensing what Jeeva was about to do, Jack bellowed, "Dude, no. We are falling in his trap by believing his words. He is playing with our mind and we are letting him win." Jeeva completely ignored Jack and continued to dig around. Jack had completely lost his sanity and the glimmer of hope he had at the start of this journey had vanished into thin air. Suddenly he heard Jeeva cry out very loudly and he turned around. Curiosity took the best of him and he started to walk towards Jeeva, his heartbeat quite erratic at that very moment. On seeing the sight in front of him, he dropped down on his knees and his deafening howls consumed the surroundings.

People at the site were discerned by the sight in front of them and they held pity for the couple in front of them. Now that the search was over, Jeeva thanked everyone who came out that day to help and immediately called the police because now the matters were to go into their hands. Within an hour or so, the police had arrived at the site and Jeeva was recounting all the incidents that had taken place, mostly defending Jack's stance. While the enquiry was progressing, Jeeva looked back to see Jack's condition but he was nowhere to be found. He was panicking mentally, just assuming the worst to have happened to his friend. He couldn't just leave to go find Jack until all the formalities were completed so he bore all the long legal procedures. As soon as that was done, he ran as fast as he could, shouting Jack's name but his panicked screams were met by no responses.

***

Jack was standing opposite Oliver, who was tied to a nearby rod pillar with ropes and was hanging two feet above the ground. They were standing in a dilapidated and run-down industry with a mere orange bulb over their heads, illuminating the entire room. The presence of the light made Oliver see clearly and fear arose within him when he saw Jack standing near a table, handling a surgical box. Meanwhile, Jack was rummaging through the box and he finally retrieved his favourite tool from the box, the surgical scalpel. He walked towards Oliver, sliding his finger on the shear side of the scalpel and just by doing that, Oliver's face turned white with dread and terror. On coming close to Oliver, he said, "She was the love of my life, you know. I loved her so much and you snatched her away from me. How sadistic are you?! What do you want? How am I supposed to live without her?!" With this, he slashed his wrist and blood spurted out, ceaselessly. He continued to ramble on, "How could you destroy her? When I saw her flesh getting decomposed, that was the end of my sanity. What did you get after killing her?" With this, he lacerated the other wrist, leaving a bloody trail all over the uneven, rumbly ground. With every drop of blood he lost, he was close to death but nothing stopped him from saying whatever was on his mind. "On seeing her lifeless body, I knew I had failed in protecting her from the evils of the world. She was gone, that too, in a blink of an eye.", Jack continued, "I am not the type of person to avenge someone's death and that is why, I forgive you, Oliver. But you have not just ended one life in your obsession, you have ended two. Remember that!" Just as he said that, he cut of one end of the rope, freeing Oliver's hand and placed a white rose in it. With one swift move, he slit across his neck and then he dropped dead, blood gashing around the place. Frightened out of his wits, Oliver freed himself from the ropes and bolted out of the place, without anyone noticing him. But he was traumatized for life because of the events that occurred in front of his eyes.

***

Two days later, Oliver was seen bundled up on the ground, shivering with trepidation. He couldn't forget the two traumatic events of his life and most importantly, he was responsible for two deaths. Two deaths were mentally torturing him every second, every minute of his passing away life that it was taking a toll over his health. He couldn't erase the agonizing memories but he couldn't struggle to live, remembering every part of it. He frantically got up from the floor and scrambled to his desk, rummaging for a paper and pen to write down his thoughts.

Dear me,

What did I do?! Why did this happen with me?! Why does God hate me?! I am a sinner, this is my punishment. I was never blessed with love, joy or success in life, instead I struggled throughout my life with the presence of sorrow, hatred and now, the guilt of killing two people, who were immensely in love with each other. I loved her. What was my mistake after all?! I was an orphan who had no significant reason to fight against the odds in order to live but she gave me that reason. My one and only reason of living was gone now because of my stupid obsession and jealousy. She accepted me as her friend in college and when that friendship did turn into love, I opened up about my feelings to her, she rejected me very politely and still continued to be my friend. But her rejection hurt me, it felt like nobody really wanted me. Finally, I decided to ghost her completely but my love or obsession for her made me stalk her yet again. When I came to know that she was in love with a guy named Jack, I went berserk crazy. I was already broken by her rejection but this pierced right through my heart. She chose someone else over me, she didn't even care about my feelings. How could she do this to me?! The fear of not being loved was eating me alive and I was losing my rationality. She should be mine and no one else's. If I couldn't have her, no one could. I waited for three years to put my plan into action but I never planned on killing Jack. It was quite unpredictable and there is nothing traumatic than seeing someone kill themselves because of you. This guilt is going to swallow me whole and I don't have any energy to crusade through the remaining part of my life. Most importantly, Jessy must be waiting for me up there. I love you, Jessy! I am coming, baby!

Yours,

Oliver

Leaving the letter on the desk, he moved to get a blade from underneath his pillow. This blade had stayed with him through thick and thin. It was time to put an end to everything. He smiled when he placed the blade vertically on his arm, preparing himself. He closed his eyes, Jessy's smiling face appearing right before him. With that image engrained in his mind, he slashed along the length of his arm, leaving a deep gash. Blood surged out, due to which he dropped down on the ground and within a few minutes, he was lying in his own pool of blood, smile still gracing his face but Oliver was gone.

YAMINI SHANKAR

"Voice Out, Women! Don't let your emotions go unheard!" ~
Yamini Shankar

From quirky quotes and captions to evocative and evolving poems and stories, she has done it all. A Supermom with a superpower to deliver brilliant yet elusive pieces of work each time her ink meets paper. Her debutant novel is in the making so be prepared to witness that in the near future. A educator, who inspires many children and nurtures them into better individuals.

Follow her on Instagram - @lanovelist

Black magic traditionally refers to the use of supernatural powers or magic for evil and selfish purposes. Very prominent practice in South India, where they perform Puja or rituals, either to benefit or harm the person in whose name the puja is performed. Once you carry out black magic, by your own or by a priest, keep in mind – **What goes around, comes around!**

Siva and Sakthi were madly in love with each other. They both shared the same interests when it came to books, songs, places to visit, etc. Although, they worked in different fields, they worked in the same premises which was convenient for the both of them to spend time together as much as possible. Both Siva and Sakthi were mature enough to understand each other's privacy and personal space, which made this relationship too good to be true. One day, Siva put forth a proposal of sticking by Sakthi's side for a lifetime and it didn't take time for Sakthi to say yes afterall. After a few years of a loving marriage, they were blessed with a girl, who they named as Sadhana, that is me, your protagonist. My dad never hesitated to fulfil every wish of mine and neither did my mom after all I was their lucky charm. It goes without saying that I love them alot.

Anyways, who exactly am I? I took an immense pride in describing myself, which not many of us would dare to do. I did, because I loved the way I was! Alright let's start, I was an above average, lean and tall girl with brown-eyes, wheatish complexion and a typical South Indian look to complete my personality. My blue and white checkered uniform, that I wore to school every morning, accentuated my look even though I looked like a nightmare by the end of the day. I came from a middle-class family where I shared the company of my parents with no siblings or relatives as such to back myself up with. I had my set of seasonal friends, little did I realise the reason behind it. You know what?! I still had one more year to break through the 12th board exam heat. I must be honest here, when it came to studies I was eggheaded, and slothful otherwise. I was a miserably jovial and an adventurous person both together. I knew no bounds in flaunting my stance if I was taken for granted. Beware okay! I took sophisticated care of my imaginary crown that kept many guys away from me (well I had the stats on the known guys, and unknown ones, I had no idea of the list), and many more were attracted to my outlook because that was what was deceptive. Everyone behind me seemed to be in a fling, not seriously wanting to get along with me (According to me! No offense). You could see me happily whiling away my time with my friends, my secret crush (Oh my god, HIM! I could see him all day), few of my seniors, who were my brothers and sisters, among whom was Rocky. I always wanted to live for the moment and in the moment, because nothing else mattered to me.

The Chance (2009):

"Okay it's late as usual! I have never been on time, man! I should be even more dedicated at least when it comes to my friends. Alright, Run Sadhana Run!", I cried out to myself and rushed soon after my dance program ended just to watch my mates' episodes. Rocky suddenly pulled me to the side, and introduced a lame guy to me.

"Hey Sadhana, this is Krish, my friend! I just thought of introducing you to each other. Bro, this is Sadhana", paused Rocky. Like me, Krish must have also been a movie buff.

He pulled off his shades to reconfirm what he saw, got captivated by my half-done makeup, I believe. Poor guy, he was assuming a lot in a fraction of seconds. Let me tell you about Krish. He was quite the average looking, not so tall, voluminous and vibrantly streaked hair, definitely not a gym hitting physique, black-eyed, brown-skinned guy. A stud in his left ear, and shades anytime of the day sported his 'I am a cool guy' look!

I gave him a strange look and said to myself, "Who on earth would wear shades at this time of the day? Looks like a buffoon!" (Thank god, I have a mind voice and that is mute almost all the time) Krish seemed to be a showoff to me, which I never like at all. "Hey Sadhana, I am currently a cabin crew trainee", Krish boasted. "Oh, I see!", I sighed in resentment. I must be honest with you, guys that the first impression of Krish spoke volumes about him being a prospective playboy.

Back then, Orkut claimed to have kept people connected and so, Krish connected to me with silly scraps like, "Hi Sadhana" "Remember me?" "We met in your school, 2 days and 16 hours before!" and this one scrap was the tip of the iceberg, "I LOVE YOU SADHANA". I was going crazy on the last sent scrap and incessantly cursing Krish, "I must get his phone number and smash him for doing this!" Unlike him, posting scrap, where everyone could see it, I send him a message privately, "Hi Krish, I want to talk to you, give me your phone number!" I thought he must have expected too much so he sent his number instantly!

I called him the next day, from a PCO near my school, with my friend standing right beside me. Someone on the other side picked up and said, "Hello!" I asked, "Who is on the line?" The guy laughed and replied, "Miss, whoever you are, you called me first, so please tell me who you are!" With this response, I definitely knew it was Krish. That's it. I started to blast out on him, "Are you insane? Don't you know the basic manners? What the hell are you getting trained as a cabin crew? Don't judge me like other girls, I don't really get carried away by your hi-fi looks and talks. In fact, I get irritated by your approach. DO NOT SPAM MY SCRAPBOOK! And goodbye!" I hung up without even giving him the chance to explain himself and then had a soda to cool myself off. With one big burp, I went home happily to eat the other snacks which my mom had filled in our fridge.

After a week of my routine schooling, I got irked when I noticed a white Hyundai Accent approaching me at quite a speed and it took a sudden break, literally making me stumble on my feet. No wonder it was Krish. He got down and as usual, removed his shades with a huge smile on his face. I was already losing my temper because he panicked me with his rash driving and now that stupid smile of his! "What do you want?", I asked him, nonchalantly. He offered me a sweet box wrapped in a pink cover and a sticker on it - **SORRY**! As soon as, I rejected it he said, "This is the last time you will see me and I wanted to apologize before that! No hard feelings!" I was a little convinced now and I accepted the sweet from him. "Remember, you should never come after me!" Saying that, I left the place.

"I like this sweet, man! It has a rose punch to it and the pink color is so beautiful. Sadly, there are only 10 pieces left. Probably, he should come back and bid one more goodbye!" I took a sneak peak through the window, it's neither cloudy nor sunny. It's unpleasant when the climate is not coordinating with my state of mind. Three days later, I called him from the same PCO, "Hi, is this Krish?" this time I had no room for his attitude and lame jokes. He responded, "Yes, Sadhana tell me. Do you want me to come near your school to pick you up?" I am astute for a moment, but I decided not to think more. Deep down, I got super excited and said, "Well if you're free, then okay!" I waited near the shop where I called him from, for around 10 minutes. I didn't have to think or even realise that he used to driving around in the neighbourhood because within 10 minutes, he was there right in front of me. For the first time ever, someone was making efforts for me, that made me ecstatic with joy. I carefully slid into his car, without giving away my excitement so that in the near future, he didn't laugh at my expense. The entire journey we didn't talk and an awkward silence engulfed our surroundings. Soon, we stopped in front of a multi-storeyed apartment. I was amused but I didn't say a word. He got onto the first floor, right side flat and knocked the door. The person who opened the door for us was obviously his mom, who shared an uncanny resemblance to Krish. I smiled at her politely and she smiled back with the same tenderness in her eyes. This was the first time I was visiting a stranger without informing my mom and I was sure my mom was going to rip me apart. Still, I didn't want to leave the place until it was too late for me.

After four months, my parents got to know that Krish and I were going out and they went for a background check on him. After which, I got to know that Krish's father had been suspended and had retired as a District Registrar (only a few, who preferred to make hay while the sun shined even in the wrong season), he got into the dirt of scam. It was not just for some land or a bribe for registration, job racketeering that's how much it is a real-time problem they faced and now they were being pushed to move out of the city, by the fuming victims. My dad spent enough time in making me understand that they were no good for me, as soon as he reached home. My mom, in this anxiety, resigned her job, just to protect me and to make me focus on my studies. None of my parents' efforts mattered to me. Or should I say, it was of no use, at the moment.

Krish's parents liked me like their daughter even though my parents hated Krish, however Krish's parents loved the idea of us getting them to elope, to move in with them to the new place they were heading to. Krish's family accompanied by me moved in together into a new place, a new city, and residence. Everything was going on pretty smoothly. I pursued my graduation from there. Amidst the chaos, my dad still took all necessary steps to find me and rescue me from the family of fascists. He cried, yelled and worried mom about me and my safety. Through the local people, who were helping Krish's family, my dad traced my whereabouts. He filed a Habeas Corpus in my locality. That was a new challenge for Krish's family about which Krish told me and warned me about the upcoming days.

To some extent, as he told me, we were taken to the police station, the enquiry went on, about my consent in staying away from my parents, mainly because I was a major, there was an enquiry. If not, the scene would have been totally different. After all the emotional tug-off war, I still chose to be with Krish, thinking that he held true intentions for me.

But as time passed by, Krish increased his command over me, he just controlled me in all aspects gradually. It was tortoise-like and not even mildly traceable that he did. I mean, he convinced me that he wasn't possessive, but he hit one of my school friends very badly and now he was afraid to talk to me. He did many such things, which made me feel, "Something was fishy!". His parents were even worse. Only sugary words came out of their mouth, they did the buttering, like a pro. Soon, I had my mind and body break down completely, where I cried almost all day without any reason, I had multiple panic attacks and anxiety issues. During the day time, I stayed numb, I hardly talked to my friends. I don't remember when I made my surroundings laugh at my undoing. I didn't focus on my studies either. Nothing mattered to me now, except sobbing and obeying him. I didn't spend time with my favourite god, Shiva anymore. I had no contacts with my parents, friends, none at all! The mental trauma was more intense at night, as the night awaited to witness my muffled sobbing. I found my surroundings terrifying because I sensed someone watching me closely when no-one was around. My room was filled with void, yet it was suffocating for me to breathe. It was a rough and soul scratching phase in my life and I could do nothing about it.

The Aroha - 2011

Though, everything that happened to me was a borderline worst-case scenario, I had one thing in that phase of my life to tranquilize. It was none other than my new best friend I could make within a matter of 6 months. My residence was a street away from Krish. I had rented and surprisingly, only my rent was taken up seriously by Krish and his parents. I don't know why. Apart from that, every other thing was casual for them. Coming back to my new best friend's announcement, she was my knight in shining armour. I got a call from my aunt, just to get to know about my vicinity and how things were progressing and I responded to her with what is what. Then I decided to call her up (my new best friend), though I was a bit scared, whether she would talk to me or not. My heart skipped a beat when she accepted my call, and said, "Tell me that you are still alive!" It pricked my heart. I continued to say, "Maa, I didn't do it deliberately! Please trust me, the situation called for this decision maa." She said, "You have no clue about what you have done to me and your dad!" I felt she was not saying, she was cursing me. And I could completely understand her pain. I added, "Maa, I myself didn't have any idea of eloping, you know me very well. My vision was completely different from what I have done now."

My mom shouted, "That is what I am unable to understand, WHY THE HELL DID YOU DO THIS?" And I had no answer for that question. I said, "Maa, what has happened has happened. I am staying in a rented apartment and I am not exploiting our culture to live with someone without marrying. So let's see how it goes maa. He is genuine with me, maa trust me." Though she was not convinced, she had no choice other than accepting whatever was going on. She said, "Take care of yourself! Talk to your dad, he is completely disappointed and upset!" I agreed and disconnected. It was such a relief to talk it out with my mother when my life was a complete mess.

The Duplicity - 2007

Two years ago...

Dino, a friend of Krish's, introduced Krish to Ananya. Krish arrived in his brand new Ford Icon to flaunt it at Ananya. Of course, she got flattered, who wouldn't. She had no knowledge that she was just studying in the 10th and it could not go any further. Krish took her to a nearby CCD, ordered Devil's Own, while Ananya thought, "Oh, man! He is flawless and he knows it all" They were having it together and she liked his company. Gradually, love blossomed between the two. Congratulations to both Ananya and Krish, because this was their first 'butterflies in the stomach' feeling. They were in their filmy phase of love. The butterflies couldn't fly for very long because Ananya's brother caught them red-handed and took them to their parents since she was too young for it.

Ananya's mother simply accepted her love at that very moment, without any sort of pleading and off-the-track after investigating came to know that Krish's background was quite shady. So she decided to play black magic tricks on Ananya to make her break up with Krish. However, Ananya knew nothing about the dark side. The powerful rituals took place with the influence of Ananya's mother. In general, no one would easily go for this option to separate silly puppy love. But the mother had to adopt this route because she got to know, through her Astrologer, that Krish had used this way to bewitch Ananya. Consequently, Ananya started to dislike Krish and wondered how did she even consider him.

Krish was clueless as to why Ananya was not attracted towards him and he started to act crazy. He tried to commit suicide, and his ever-sweet Horlicks mom took his horoscope to the astrologer and got to know what was wrong. She was shocked to know that her effort was counteracted and her pampered spoiled brat was trapped by black magic. Maybe now is the time, she realized the sequel of **"What goes around, comes around"**

Hence, she decided to adopt the same weapon. She fired back and Ananya's knees went weak. Ananya came back to Krish, within the blink of an eye. Ananya's mom, no less than her opponent, fired back since her daughter's life was dearly valuable to her and wanted to shape her life for the better. Ananya and Krish were fooled by their beloved mothers in the name of the Black Magic War. After the trial and her board exams, she was put in a residential school for her higher education as advocated by her mother. One fine day, Ananya and Krish would finally realize that the butterflies in their stomach were no more.

The Aroha - 2011 *(Contd.)*

"I got to know all these from Dino, who recently happened to realize what he has done to Ananya. He felt really bad for her, but luckily Ananya is out of the picture and now with me in the frame, we surely have to do something, Maa!" My mom, like other moms, was a super mom. Whatever the situation might be, she always came to my rescue. My dad, on the other hand, was very strong physically as well as emotionally. I presumed that he must have been made up of rocks and stones. Just thinking about my situation, he didn't get proper sleep. The next morning, dad asked me to meet him at a hidden location.

Later that day, I visited my dad in the said place, with eyes of Judas Iscariot, pathetic and vulnerable. My dad consoled me knowing how much I am going through off-late. He offered me filter coffee and biscuits though I didn't want to eat, I took two just because I didn't want to make him feel bad anymore. He initiated the conversation and got to the point of how and why he felt that way. Soon, I left for home. I walked back home, reflecting on why my dad sounded interrogative today. I also felt happy that my Knight and King made all efforts to keep me calm and composed.

I was sure that after today's conversation, my dad had this gut feeling of me being trapped by black-magic and witchcrafts. Because he had seen his sister go through it and get out of it after facing the same rhythmic troubles and mental issues in her life. Every good had a little of bad in it and vice versa. If black-magic was bad and a threat, there were some people who'd heal and fight back the black-magic and dark spirits. That's how my dad's sister could help herself when she was trapped by one. My dad tried to talk about this and convinced me to go to a place where they healed people who could have been tricked by the influence of witchcraft. I was a 3rd generation girl and obviously no significant amount of evidence would make me believe in anything called **black-magic**. After I recollected whatever I had said, and I brooded over the changes my life had undergone, my state became worse than ever. I was left with no option except to listen to my king.

One day, my dad without any notice, took me to a temple, and there I met the chief priest and the healer who made me do the ritual, once in every ten days. The priest didn't pester me unlike Krish, thank god. He asked me to go around the temple, recite a few mantras, be a true believer and devote myself to social activities, like serving food, cleaning the remains without any hesitation. He asked me to consider all these a way to reach my destiny, philosophically and not spiritually. I liked this one genuinely because once you start tolerating whatever bothers you, or whatever is out of your style, you master it. Gradually, I felt much better and started to understand things. After a couple of days, once I felt good, my dad slowly educated me about what Krish's parents had done to my life, I could feel my knees go weak and I was scared to death. When I thought of how I was going to get engaged to Krish, my heart just stopped beating for a moment, thinking that I deserved to die than go through with this. But still, I was hesitant to believe, though I had already gotten a glimpse and a flavour of the situation, I just couldn't process it in, because deep down I believed Krish had true intentions for me and his efforts were genuine.

One late afternoon, when I came back from college pretty early, I observed a priest coming out of the home. He had big hair and a long beard with a kumkum stretch on his forehead, adorning all kinds of necklaces and bracelets. In fact, only after seeing this appearance, I was able to relate to what Kasturi ma explained and why I did those rituals. I was restless, not knowing what my next action ought to be. I called up my dad directly without involving my mom first.

"Appa, I saw someone going into my place and walking out when I reached home from college. I am scared to go inside, paa. Please tell me what to do.", I screamed feebly on my phone.

"Nothing to panic, kutty, (he comforted me by calling "kutty" often reminding me of my mom calling me "pattu" and the moment I listen to these, I have tears in my eyes). Get into your home but do not touch anything strange there, just look for something unusual and I am coming there in an hour." My dad always did his best. Trust me!

I walked into my home, keenly and carefully scanning everything. I found meat flesh, my hair and a lemon all tied up together, looking terrifying and awkward in my cupboard. I felt like puking right away. My dad rang the bell, and I ran like I was going to rescue myself. As soon as I saw him through the door, I felt at home. He rushed to the thing that was kept in my cupboard, and started educating me that this will mesmerize me and keep me hooked with Krish, come what may. I felt shattered because I still believed that everything happened naturally with him and it was going to last forever. But everything was a set-up, by some mere bloody rituals? These rituals changed me so much? How could someone ruin someone else's life just by reciting and practicing tricks? Why was God so unfair with these mean people? There were a stream of questions running in my mind. Yet I tried to answer each one of them and move along. At one point, I could connect all the dots and there I was. Going back to my pavilion. Sadhana was a warrior! She stopped at nothing!

The Crux - 2013

I waited patiently till I graduated. Till then, I had successfully managed to convince Krish and his parents to wait for our engagement. I completed my final semesters, results were declared and I had aced the exam. I was a graduate now. Again, they started talking about the engagement just like any other South Indian melodramatic movie. I was restless, not knowing what my next move should be. I went to my room, sat and contemplated over everything. I finally decided to run away from the house so I called my knight and told her my decision. She always supported my actions and she got prepared. It was 03:00 am, I walked off with my back-pack, rushed to "my own Home Sweet Home", hugged my parents so tight that I cried for hours together. Both of them were waiting for me to come out of the trauma and then I started to explain all of this. Weird flex and twist, right? Well, it was time to break it down then. Krish and his family weren't just a part of a random corruption, job racketing scam or bribery. They went a step ahead and dived into the indulgence of black magic and witchcraft. So that's how shit got real for me, soon after tasting pink sweet. You remember the rose flavoured sweet? That's how I fell head over heels in love with Krish instead of hating him or easily getting bored of him, that's how I gradually started changing my character towards him, they were the real witchcraft experts. And yes, that's how I easily moved in with them, that's how I took all of their orders, that's how I became a submissive for Krish and that's how I had all these anxiety issues, panic attacks, and all the mental health breakdowns.

Despite me running away from there and coming back to my peaceful void, I had another surprise in store for me - I was pregnant. I was going crazy, not knowing what my next move will be. I thought that this will become my favourite mantra eventually. I now regretted visiting him. Again, it was because of his parents, since they had insisted. I was helpless and felt like screaming out the tears, agony, betrayal, failure, hatred that I have felt for the past so many years. I wanted to isolate myself now and forever.

I had seen girls, who would easily switch between multiple relationships. And those girls got married like a princess. I had always been a princess to my dad and mom, I had been too sincere in my relationship, I had not ditched anyone in the name of love. My parents nourished me with honesty, innocence and some courage that helped me survive the evils of the world. I wanted to kill myself for ruining my life without anyone's influence, all by my own. Unlike those who blamed their boyfriends for ruining their lives, I was ashamed and blamed myself. A cheap, filthy sweet collapsed my life completely. I had big goals, I wanted to explore all that I could. I fulfilled none of my parents' wishes nor mine. With all the emotions suppressed air-tight in my heart, I slowly came back to my senses, and thought of how Krish had always been calculative and manipulative towards me. His insecurity had pushed me to become a mother, when I had not even seen what the outside world was ready to offer me. I must admit, without my Knight and King, I would have been unable to breathe in this pollution. "Man, I don't really deserve this! I had never harmed anyone, then why did it happen to me?" I still couldn't convince myself that out of all the bad girls around, I had to deal with such disturbing events when I probably do not even deserve. I pondered, sitting against the window, cursing myself every now and then. Through the window, saw the sky, too dim for me, conveying a subtle melancholy.

The Heavy Duty - 2020

The Present

I am not a college student anymore, as a matter of fact, I am a Team Leader at a top-notch MNC company and a single mom. Don't be suspicious whether or not, I was inviting any more trouble by the name of Krish. I know no bounds in being myself now. I could feel all of the six senses in perfect accordance. I am back with my charisma, which indeed has always been my backbone. My life is smooth and good now after all, I have been through a lot for the past few years. I somehow survived to break free from the battles because any girl of my age would have killed herself mercilessly after finding out that she is pregnant, especially when the relationship was on the verge of sinking! The sky is bright, clear and it feels indicative to me. Alright, nothing can be done as a counteract. After a lot of mental fighting, stress and depression, I am content about the baby, as it knows no harm, and it is inhumane to kill the baby just to get her life better. Needless of convincing, my parents are ready to stand by my side, along with the beautiful soul growing within my womb to fight against all the odds life has to offer. So they decided to heal The Womb and The Wound!

Confession Time:

This story is based on true events! May we never take a chance on this trick as a shortcut to reach our destination. This is momentary and not permanent. Do not toss someone's life to flourish yours! Do not encourage others pertaining to the same. It ruins just as "What goes around, comes around". Sadhana was a teenager when she got trapped in this maze. All the more, she was a vivid girl, who had big goals to achieve and reach heights. However, none of her wishes came true, because her important phase of life was busy in clearing the bushes. She had no clue that she would become a mother at the age of 20! And the Wound suffered for the same as much as the Womb did. It caused real pain, you know! So please be *wary that **The Harm You Set is the Harm You Get!** Remember anything that comes instant, goes away at an instant. So choose wise and grow it gradually, be it anything!*

RIYA DEEPAK BANKA

"Only some mere excuses can stop us from following our dreams." ~ Riya Deepak Banka

A Housewife, who has taken her passion to great big levels and is definitely adding an edge to the world of writing. From being the Author of a self published book to working on a few anthologies at the moment, she has done it all. Life has taught her so many lessons, which you will realise when you take a sneak peak of her writings.

Follow her on Instagram - @riyadeepakbanka

"Rabia is having an affair with Ansh!"

A message, which changed the years to come, forever. A message, whose arrival had its own set of repercussions, for which I had not prepared. This message entered into my life on a late evening, when I was busy in enjoying my birthday party and hosting my guests. Exactly at 6:30pm, every girl's phone at the party simultaneously beeped signalling a new message to which they immediately checked their phones to read the text after which, all eyes were on me. Some of them looked at me with jealousy and disdain, while others looked at me with pity filled eyes.

Who was Ansh, you ask? Ansh was my best friend at school. We had been friends since primary school. Our friendship was quite platonic and we were too comfortable around each other, that often gave people the wrong message. Everyone at school did have their doubts regarding our relationship but since the message happened, doubts had been confirmed and rumours had started to go around, about the relationship that never existed. Each and everyone was gossiping about the message and about us, and nothing was the same anymore.

Helplessly, I looked around the place to see the damage that one text had caused and to rectify it, I kept calling the unknown number which was unfortunately switched off. I was getting frustrated by the minute as my birthday turned into a nightmare for me. My phone kept blinking with unending calls and texts of all the people who wanted to get some dirt on the text and the truth behind it. I glanced at Ansh to see him anxious and tensed about the situation because in a way, this had jeopardised our 14 year long relationship. He sensed me looking at him and looked over, giving me empathetic looks and reassuring me that things will die down.

Ironically, in a world full of advanced technology, there was no way of finding out who sent that message because the sender had covered his tracks up really well. The only option left for me was to lodge a police complaint but I knew that what came next was even nastier than this, confronting my parents about Ansh. I was the victim but no one would have believed me.

It is often said that ignorance is a bliss and I ignored the text altogether because I knew there was no way out other than this. The world and the society we live in never lets you move forward from your past and the same happened with me. Next day was a school day, a hell lot convenient for the gossip mongers of my school, who wanted on every bit of details of Ansh and my relationship. Ansh too, was equally hesitant about the whole episode that was supposed to entail the time we would enter school. He told me about the list he was preparing in order to pinpoint the sender and the conclusion we reached was that it could be anybody, anyone from school or even outside. But why would someone go to such an extent to harass us. Every single minute that passed by, I only thought of one thing, what exactly did I do to be on the receiving end of such a wildfire.

On entering the gates of the school, all eyes were on me and people kept whispering stuff into each other's ears with looks of shock, contempt and sympathy as if I had committed a crime. I stayed low and passed by everyone in the hallway, without sparing a glance because I didn't know how long I could contain my anguish and grief at the judgemental looks that I kept getting for a stupid, false text. As days passed, I made peace with whatever had happened and tried to move on for the better but I didn't know that it was the calm before the storm. The storm arrived exactly two months later at midnight when Ansh called me and spat out in one breath, tension wavering in his voice, "Rabia! Get up and check your Facebook account right now. Someone has hacked into your profile." "What the hell?! Ansh, please tell me you are joking!", I shouted, anxiety taking the best of me and my trembling hands reached out for my laptop and I frantically typed to get into my account. Password incorrect! Even the third time was in vain. This could only mean someone had completely taken over my social media life and changed the password too.

"Hello! Hello! Rabia? Dude, where are you lost?", Ansh shouted through the phone, thinking the worst had happened to me. "Ansh, my password has been changed for my Facebook account and I can't even access my email too. Send me the screenshots of what exactly is going on my profile.", I responded, my voice wavering with angst. My phone beeped just 5 mins later and as soon as the pics got downloaded, shock was quite an understatement of what I was feeling. Ten screenshots of the Messenger chat between Ansh and I. The chat was entirely based on both of us sexting which also contained obscene pictures of both of us. This was not possible at all as the only thing we have exchanged on Messenger is memes, not even texts as we didn't trust social media platforms after past incidents. Even reading the chats made me feel disgusted and tears were threatening to make its way down my cheeks now. How could things go to such an irreparable extent? I was shivering intensely whilst tears fell onto my mobile screen.

This was what people called a living nightmare. My character was at stake here because I was sure that people would not believe that this was fake and someone was harassing me. My phone blared, startling me out of my thoughts and I saw that Ansh was calling me again. He said that he tried his best to recover my password but he had failed do so he asked his friend, Karan to help out. Karan was the tech whiz of our class who had a great knowledge of how things work in the network world. After asking me some security questions related to my account, he disconnected leaving me to my unnerving thoughts.

What if Karan was also not able to wipe out my account? How many people had seen that post? If things didn't settle by the time morning came, suicide will be the only option. No sliver of hope, I could see about this situation and I was slowly dying inside, realising the aftermath of the post. Through a mere Facebook account, this cyber criminal had taken over my life and had created a mayhem. After a while, I saw an unknown number calling me. I hesitated before picking it up and answering with a 'Hello'. "Hey Rabia, it's me, Karan. I asked for your number from Ansh. Are you okay? Don't worry, I will make sure that all traces of the post and your account are wiped away as soon as possible. Just hold on, don't lose hope.", Karan reassured me. "Thank you, Karan and I owe it to you. You are doing me the greatest favour.", I responded, with emotion laced in my voice which he noticed and immediately said, "Okay, I am going and getting things done. You just relax!" Once he had disconnected, I sighed in relief, just thinking about how Karan didn't know me personally too well but he was ready to help out, just because I was Ansh's best friend. I had rejected him the past too and still, he was ready to help me. I sat down to pray to the Gods to save whatever shred of reputation and self-respect was left, even after the text and the post.

I felt an immense pain erupt in my chest as I felt someone stabbing me in the heart multiple times. The one thought that I couldn't dismiss since the text happened was 'Who was the person behind all this?' and 'What did I do to hurt this person so badly that my sheer consequences have led to my undoing?' But no one in particular popped up in my mind who would have so much hatred for me to turn my life upside down.

Half an hour later, Karan called to tell me that my account was deleted, which made me take a sigh of relief and I thanked him several times. I still knew that those who saw the post would start a wildfire about it and the repercussions were coming my way when I go to school in the morning. But, that was the least of my concerns because I couldn't shake off the feeling of who could the culprit be, for a moment I thought it was Ansh but I was a witness to his tech skills and they were poorly bad plus, he was my best friend, who would never do something like this to hurt me.

Like it is usually said, this was just a trailer of what the future had in store for me, things were not ending anytime soon. In the days that came, I received text messages displaying a shady company's name which sent links to obscene websites and a few numbers were attached to the text. They were vile and filthy and to some extent, frightening too because this came as a threat. Is there anything more vicious than this left for me to go through? The worst part was that my closed ones didn't know what I was going through, especially my parents. When it came to building up the courage to tell my parents what exactly my life was becoming, I was at my wit's end. I came from a conservative family, where ideals and principles were the basis for everything. The aftermath of me divulging all the mayhem would not work out very well for me and instead I will be grounded for life and I will not be allowed to take any legal action.

The only lead I had after the text, post and the threat was that my cyber criminal was a male and this I was sure of. What scared me was that if I do approach the legal officers about my situation, I wouldn't really get justice. On the other hand, I may even been framed for bringing this on myself and the trauma of legal action will take a toll over my life. The only sensible thing I could do was to ignore the threat altogether and move on forward in life. I also convinced my parents to get me a new sim and when they did ask me the reason for the same, I was forced to give an excuse.

Gradually, I was losing every part of me and I had become a very lifeless soul. I had cut off all connections with my batchmates and friends even Ansh. He tried a lot to get me out of my shell and to talk to me on several occasions but I completely shunned him away. For a long time, I stopped using my phone too and tried to seek help but no one could provide me with a solution to the chaotic mess my life was in. I was just sick of hearing them say 'Ignore it and move on!' and 'Just be patient!' and 'You are not alone, it will pass!'.

These three statements did not help in reassurance at all, moreover as time passed, I became a victim of depression.

Time flew by so fast that soon I was done with my board exams and I was heading to Delhi for my higher studies. Before I left, I made sure that I broke all ties with everyone who knew about my past. This time, I truly wanted a fresh start and I wanted to escape my past so badly that I played safe. Except for Whatsapp, I opted out of every social media platform which my parents found weird but they were happy that their daughter was finally becoming mature and thinking about her future (according to them, social media destroys a person's career).

New me, new place, new friends and a whole new atmosphere, yes I thought that my past was not coming back to haunt me anymore but somewhere at the back of my mind, I knew it wasn't the last of my miseries. Was the person waiting for the right time?! Maybe, Maybe not!

Peace prevailed once again in my life or so I thought until the day came. A beautiful Monday morning became a disastrous one within the span of a few minutes. I got a call from my cousin who bellowed at me for posting indecent pictures and captions. I was lost obviously, thinking as to where this was coming from as I definitely did not post any picture anywhere. No social media, remember?! I disconnected the call and borrowed my roommate's phone to see what the fuss was all about. As soon as I typed my name and clicked on my profile, I was stunned would be quite an understatement to say. What with a new start when your past comes trailing from behind and attaches on like a leech, never to leave? A picture of me and a batchmate, that too presumably a cropped group photo with the following caption 'I sleep with him every single day!'. How was this even possible?! This was my profile picture on Whatsapp. Something was definitely amiss here because I did not share my number with anyone back in my hometown. Didn't Karan delete my profile? What I was sure of was one thing and that was, anything platonic could be made to look obscene or trashy on social media and people have ulterior motives behind it. It had been a year since I opened my Facebook account but none of my Facebook friends noticed that my account had been hacked into. What was blasphemous was that people were actually liking that picture and it spread like wildfire.

The one number that my brain couldn't get rid of was Ansh's and so I called him, hoping I could put an end to it. On picking up the call, he informed me that he was already on it and Karan was trying to figure out how did my account reactivate. That very moment, I broke down in front of him, not knowing what to say or do and he kept cooing gently, reassuring me that things will not get out of hand anymore. I thanked him profusely for his timely help and cut the call. By this time, I knew that all my family members would be aware of the ruckus in my life and that scared me a lot because I did not know what their reaction would be. Just a few mins later, my phone vibrated in my hand and I was horrified to see my brother calling me. Did he know?! I hesitatingly picked up the call and answered with a 'Hello'. "Rabia, hey are you okay? I was stunned to see your Facebook post today but I knew that you would never post anything like that because my Rabia is not like that.", my brother asked, with a tensed voice. I knew then and there that I should have opened the pandora's box when I had the opportunity because my biggest support system in these tough times was my family. I broke down miserably on the call, barely able to speak. He tried to calm me down but all his efforts were in vain. Since the post had happened, my inbox had been flooded with messages and calls from my batchmates, college friends, school friends and everyone who had seen the trending post of mine. I wanted to throw my phone at the wall so that I could stop the incessant ringing but I was too tired to even take out my frustration, I had finally given up. I needed fresh air and a cigarette to forget about all the inhibitions and chaos around me. Staying on the seventh floor of the hostel was definitely elevating because the view was beautiful. I stood on the edge of the balcony, puffing out smoke now and then, just reflecting upon the crisis at hand. In that very moment, things became clearer and the story had thus manifested itself in my mind. The hacker was not smart after all and that was more than enough for me to figure out why did this all start. I should have guessed it sooner but dumb luck. I went back to my study table and starting scribbling a note, mentioning each and every single thing from the text on my birthday to today's post. This sheet of paper was the wanted climax to my story because who would trust a girl and punish a guy. I was not ready to become a victim again and definitely not ready to let anyone into my mind, I was past all that and I had to react on this as soon as possible. I returned back to the balcony with a genuine smile on my face, which I thought would never resurface. I finished my cigarette but instead of throwing the bud, I jumped off the balcony taking it with me.

Was I dead or alive, you'd ask?! Well I was alive, although I was put in a medically induced coma so that my body repaired itself in the meanwhile. Two months had gone by and the day came when I regained my consciousness. Multiple fractures and countless stitches later, I lay wide awake in the hospital bed, staring intently at the ceiling. Through the corner of my eye, I saw my parents walk in with my brother and Ansh following from behind. My plan had certainly worked and I had the strength to ask just this one question, "Where is Karan?" They looked at one anther apprehensively, after which my dad spoke up, "He is in jail. Everything is over, Rabia. You have nothing to be worried about."

Confused?! Let's rewind back to the day my profile got hacked for the second time. Remember, I had asked my roommate for her phone to check the post?! That very moment when I was frantically typing my name to see the post on Facebook, a Whatsapp notification had popped up. It was a message from 'Karan Bhaiya', the same Karan from my hometown presumably. How did I know this, you ask?! Priya was actually from my hometown and she actually empathized with me in my situation but I did not know that she was Karan's cousin sister. The reason was crystal clear now as to why Karan tortured me all along. He had a crush on me in school but like the rest of our batch, he too thought that Ansh was my boyfriend. One thing was clear that other than Priya, no one here or even back in my hometown had my phone number. No one other than Priya would have shared my profile picture. The tech whiz of our class, had momentarily fooled me by merely deactivating the account to gain my trust but he did give away his cover by messaging his sister.

The note, where I had poured my heart out and highlighted every detail of the crime, was my trump card. I knew that if I would have told my parents about everything, they would've not allowed me to take it to the legal authorities but if I involved the police in some way, they would have to go to the bottom of the story. I know that a year had passed by with traumatic experiences along the way but what was far important was that I was mentally recovering and slowly gaining my inner peace of mind.

JOYE DUTTA

"Express your thoughts through the art of writing and in the process, explore yourself, you will definitely be surprised by the outcome." ~ **Joye Dutta**

An ingenious photographer with the brilliant skill of bringing her snaps come to life with succinct captions and quotes. Bringing an unhackneyed aspect of romance, she can't resist adding a sublime amount of tragedy to her pieces. Romance genre is her 'claim to fame' genre where she makes you live her characters through her stories.

Follow her on Instagram - @joyedutta13

You remember the first time we met, it was in my Literature Major's class. You entered the classroom and saw me smiling. As far as I recall we had met before but this was the first time only, we actually had a full-on conversation, that too when I made you read my poem and you said and I quote 'I usually don't like it when people say they write poems because it always ends up in me reading mediocre writings but this one is a masterpiece, you do write really well and you definitely should show me a few more of your write-ups when we meet next'. I was flushed with happiness as that was the first time anyone complimented my skill so beautifully.

17 September, our first of the many times, we had a really long whatsapp conversation when you responded to my story which was a poem again. You were the only one who could understand the meaning and depth of my words. Inquisitiveness took over me as I wanted to know you better and understand your wants, likes-dislikes and everything about you. That was an unexpected emotion I felt when I was talking to you because your compliments were not about my pretty face or the perfect cheekbones I had, they were purely about the way I write and the way I describe my emotions in very little words, which meant the world to me when you appreciated my feelings and thoughts.

***

Next few days, you skipped coming to college. I remember you telling me you were 21 and I was 17 and that you're a person who sticks to his words. You also declared unapologetically to keep some distance and that was quite unusual to see nowadays with boys.

You ordered me not to ask about your parents. You were an honest man who was suffering from bipolar disorder and extreme mood swings but tremendously cared for the people you loved. You had hurt every single person who loved you and maintaining relationships was not your cup of tea. Oh! I remember you told me about her, the one who dared to love you but you shattered her. You said you loved her after she took off from your life so why didn't you apologize for your behavior? May be, you didn't want her to get hurt again because you loved her truly. From 'loving truly', do you remember your 1st year relationship?! You told me about that bi**h, sorry for my language but I couldn't take it when I saw your devastated, broken self. No reason to spare even for your closure, I mean, is that how relationships end these days?! You were crazily in love with her and I recall you once said, "She was the best kiss you'd ever had, both passionate and wild." Your friends had been your support system at that time and had witnessed you at your lowest. Crying and hugging your friends all night was how you got over her somehow. Quite relatable at my end because I too had gone through a similar situation in my life too, where this guy bet that he could make me fall in love with him. Naïve me fell hard, not just once but four times. Anyways, let's not talk about that miserable 4 year period of my life.

***

Our late night chats, where we explicitly talked about our dark days, made me pen down my feelings on my notepad,

For you...

I saw him standing, through the hurricane in the past...

Everything was broken but no one could bend his mast...

He was abundant but gave demons his home...

Lost everything and became a thunderstorm...

Love made him strong, attachment makes him weak...

Days made him hide, nights made his talent to out seek...

We made him silent, he helped himself to speak...

joyedutta13

And the next thing, I know is that I sent it to you eagerly awaiting for you to say something. Yeah, you did say something which I'll never forget. "Honestly, I'm amazed. Only one word – Love. Literally, best thing I have read in a very long time", you paused for a moment and continued to ramble on, "Who's your inspiration for this? A friend, brother, father? Whoever it is, this piece is absolutely phenomenal." I replied, "You're the inspiration!" A moment passed with no reply from your end, which made me think, maybe you got offended but then you responded, "I feel honoured and grateful because I'm not really a person, who is a muse for someone's poems. I am kinda like a villain or an anti-hero at best so this is definitely new for me. Anyways, I love this poem of yours." Underestimating yourself was something you used to do very often but I really wished if you had seen yourself from my eyes just once.

***

Cheers to one month of togetherness! During the day, there were times we didn't meet each other but the nights were what I yearned for the most because of the night long conversations ranging from abstract topics to contemporary ones. I felt attached to you through those chats.

Exactly two days later 19th October, I cannot forget this date as it was your birthday. I was really excited to celebrate it with you as I was the only one invited with 3 other seniors. I wanted to gift you something that will always remind you of my existence, something very special and unique and obviously cute (You know, I love cute things). In addition to the gift, I decided to write a letter to you talking about all those times you helped me when no one listened to me, all those times you consoled me whenever I was downright depressed, all those times you teased me saying I am a Kid. Summing up everything within two pages was going to be difficult because the things you'd done for me couldn't be limited to two pages. As you loved to read my poems, I wrote one for you in that letter too.

I remember that, on entering the café, you were the first one my eyes searched for. My eyes fell on your jacket, one of the apparels that I love to see you in and headed towards your direction. I shyly wished you a 'Happy Birthday' and then gave you your gift, nervous as hell whether or not you will like it. Now that I recall, there was a genuine smile on your face when you held my present in your hand, which made my heart swoon with happiness. As I was not a people person, I usually used to resort to using my mobile phone, which you clearly disliked so I refrained from doing it that day and gave you my undivided attention. But I realized that I enjoyed spending time with you more than I did with my phone. From your smiles to your sarcastic jokes to your secret glances, everything made the time spent together unforgettable.

***

The month was coming to an end with only 4 days left and then that day came which was a major surprise for me. At exactly, 2:45am, we shared our first 'I Love You'. Yeah, I had really strong intimate feelings for you and I believe that moment was intimate for the both of us. Was I aware of the consequences that were to come in the future? Yes, I did because it was you who I dared to love. Someone who couldn't maintain relationships because of his bipolar personality with excessive mood swings but even after that, my feelings were my trump card. But I would've never imagined that the start of something new could end in 4 days. 4 days! Completely taken aback by the duration of our relationship, I still was in denial but it was your choice and I respected that so I didn't force you. You left me but your memories stuck by and I always lived to see the flashbacks of all the times we spent together.

***

With you, things were spontaneous. One moment, you left me, making me resort to loneliness without our habitual night chats and now look, here we are again, with your message, which was a screenshot of my poem and a text that said something along the lines that my words were cruel.

You're a person who inspired me every moment of my life, and then one day, I was inspired by the inspirations you gave me. But this time, I felt devastated and my thoughts went on spewing the brutal feelings it was going through.

Ⓟⓗⓐⓢⓔⓢ

I can't keep you for life, you're a seasonal wind...

You didn't just stop by touching my soul, but letting me feel sinned...

I tried to hold you close to me, but you escaped out of it...

Came with a flourishing spring with you and left the world of tind...

joyedutta13

We started talking again, not like we usually did but I knew that this texting is not stopping anytime soon. You did ask me to leave but you also asked me to send my write-ups because you loved reading them. You warned me that you had no feelings left for me, but I knew that wasn't true at all. I sensed the underlying care and concern you had for me underneath that tough exterior which was still in denial. Our chats, crazy and stupid was something that you looked forward to, I know this but you were a man who had so many reasons but none to spare. You'd say and I quote 'I have my reasons! But I'll not tell you!' It was hilarious as this was your standard or more like default reply to any prying question of mine.

***

By the end of the year, we were knee-deep in conflicts, always arguing about you staying when you clearly didn't want to. We had our own set of bad days, just figuring out what went wrong. Even on New Year's eve, when I wished you a 'Happy New Year' with an emoji, I was left on seen and a cold New Year wish graced my phone next morning. I remember you telling me you love Christmas and you celebrated it with great joy. That was one of the times, you let me into your life by sending me pictures of the decorations, food, Christmas tree and of course, Lucy, your cat, your 3 am friend and the only one who truly makes you happy. "Where's my gift for Christmas?", I texted you to which you replied back, "You're not qualified for that, nobody from the college is in my list" with a never-mind emoji. I knew you were not very connected in college with your batchmates but I still decided against it and stuck to my question. "I want a gift. As you are celebrating, you should give me a gift." You ignored my text and just changed the topic and as usual, I just went with the flow. That night, we texted a lot and discussed about the upcoming BLF (Bhopal Literature Festival). I remember you going alone for the event on the very 1st day and sending me pictures of the amazing things that happened. Then we made plans to go together or should I say, be there together and enjoy the event. On reaching the event venue, I saw you standing behind the waterfall, checking out the schedule for the day and quickly glancing at your phone time to time, which made me realize you were waiting for me.

The day couldn't have been better spent if I did not have your company every step of the way. From listening to literary artists and performances to enjoying the tea while watching the sunset, every moment was just so beautiful. We stayed there till 7:00pm and then decided to leave so that I could reach my house on time. We walked to your scooty together as you offered to drop me home and I loved that feeling. You had a strong feeling for me, which I could sense through your way of communication. "You should know how to make fun of the things you love the most (and you did make fun of me then)", you said but paused for a minute and then stated, "You'll not understand it!" But I understood what you meant by that, after all I could feel you breath deeply. You never touched me except for the hand shake, but my heart was flipping like crazy by that small gesture.

***

On the way to my house, you wished to eat and you wanted to do so with me as you wanted to remember the day. This gesture made me immensely happy but as I was both time-bound and money-bound, I couldn't cater to your wishes and my desires. Just as we had been seated on the scooty, you remarked "A baby could easily fit in between us" when you saw me sitting at the edge of the scooty seat. I was shocked because I wanted to sit closer to you but with you, I never knew what would the outcome be. Anyways, I came closer and I could feel the heat of your neck. The sharp feature of your back didn't help my heart which was beating excessively today and urging me to kiss you on your neck. I sat stifled, merely listening to you talk animatedly and enjoying the cold winter air hitting my face as you rode at a slow speed that evening. That was definitely not the last time I sat on your scooty as we attended the last two days of BLF together too. But the most memorable and surprising incident of the last day was when you stopped by the café to eat out but I relentlessly refused and tricked you into changing the direction of your scooty (unfortunate turn of events). In that ride back home, I realized how you made me fearless of going out with you and returning home late even though I should be more careful (blame crime tv serials for this thought)

****

What happened to you after BLF?! Why'd you distance yourself from me?! You completely pushed me into the seen-zone with no reasons. Then one fine day, you text me "Don't text me again and You are to not meet me anymore!" Yeah, your mood swings had kicked in which is what I thought but me being my stubborn self, didn't want to leave you alone, neither could I let you go without you giving me reasons but the blue ticks were the responses to all my texts that day. The next few days, no messages, no pictures graced my phone from your end and that left me with an unbearable pain of being clueless as to what went wrong this time.

I described my situation by writing and this time too, I wrote something for you...

What should I cry for and what I should be happy about...

You became a beautiful part of my routine, yet you'll fade away someday I doubt...

I know our fate, thus I remained silent when I wanted to shout...

Our roads will be separated but how can we smile I try to figure it out...

We know we're bad at goodbyes, but we'll share our last words and will disappear in the crowd...

I hope there is sometime left for us, just stay right now...

joyedutta13

***

Out of nowhere, you attended college one day and I noticed you walking towards my seniors, from the bench of the college canteen that I had occupied. Unfortunately, on that day I was alone as my friends were absent so I was buried into my diary, writing as you see. You were smiling and talking to my seniors, which made me smile too but I realized that you wanted me out of your life so I just turned my back to you. I knew you looked at my back because I could sense someone watching but for once, I didn't feel like blushing at all, I was upset by your aloof and distant self.

That very afternoon of 12th November 2019, when I was busy absorbing the sights from the window of my bus, a message popped up on my vacant screen.

"I never apologized for loving someone, I know I have hurt your feelings………." the rest of the message was a blur because my eyes welled up and tears threatened to fall out at any moment. The message cleared one thing that you loved me but I was not good enough for you to keep. Though you never wanted to hold onto anyone, but I did and I badly wanted to hold onto you.

Your message gave me a moment of happiness as well as sadness and the overthinking and misery led the treacherous teardrop make its way down my face, matching the rhythm of the bus. Surprising it seems, I couldn't feel any emotion anymore after my heart had calmed down.

***

Two days later, I got to know that you'll be leaving the state permanently and will shift to Hyderabad for your further studies, after which you will depart from India forever, leaving behind tons of memories in the hearts of your beloved ones.

I was in shock and, depression had engulfed me. I could feel my head becoming heavier by the minute and the pain in my diaphragm and throat made me realize that I was unable to cry. I was just thinking about the days we had spent during the Literature Festival, one of the most memorable days of my life till date after your birthday, of course. I started to realize that everything would never be the same anymore, I'll never be able to admire you from afar or even listen to you talk or click your pictures or walk beside you or even feel the sun drowning inside the water leaving a beautiful crimson color in the sky with the slow cold breeze touching your face and coming onto mine.

***

I felt suffocated in my own room. I couldn't help myself from opening my whatsapp and typing out a message to which I didn't expect anything in return.

"I love you!"

You instantly came online, and replied, "I know and I understand it's hard for you but for your sake, just move on. You'll be alright in some time." You did write a few more lines but I couldn't hold myself back anymore and I broke into tears. For a moment, I thought I'll be fine after a while but these days, nothing seemed to be right anymore. After a few of my text messages, you said, "From now on, don't text me!" Sitting on my bed with your text message glaring at my face, I wrote my final response to you, "I'll try!"

PALLAVI KAPIL

"I am a Dreamer who believes that without Emotion, Drama and Humour, a piece of expression is amiss." ~ **Pallavi Kapil**

From the snow-cladded valleys of Himachal, a young bilingual poet who loves to express through her words and create an impact. Our poet can usually be seen doing either of these things – talking to complete strangers about their experience or getting up on stage and performing poetry!

Follow her on Instagram - @pallavi_writes

"Padhe to nahin, par kadhe zaroor hain beta!", Amma said while wiping the tears off her eyes. What she said translates to '*We haven't studied but we surely are simmered with experiences, child.*'

"Oh Amma, you're so emotional!", I laughed at her melodramatic stance while she was preoccupied in cleaning her bifocal glasses.

And stupid too! I wanted to add but didn't.

"I am happy that my kids (dad and aunt) were able to provide all those facilities to their kids (us), which I failed to provide them as a parent....", she continued to ramble on. With every word, her emotions took the best of her and now she was full on crying over the same things, I got busy in observing her expressions, body language and catching onto her one liners so that I could laugh at them later. Whenever she cried, her lips drooped down like a wilted leaf and her eyebrows lifted up like the cornice of a mountain. I didn't know her age, but the wrinkles over her sun baked face and the sodium chloride colour of her tresses indicated that she was old. Amma, my grandmother didn't live with us. She lived in Mangla in her father's ancestral house, which she had inherited from him. She used to visit us once in a week. She'd come on Sunday evening, stay overnight and leave for Mangla the next morning. On her trip to Mangla, she was accompanied by *Laali* and *Bhuri*, her cows.

'*Why doesn't Amma live with us? Why does she cry all the time?*' I'd always wonder.

'*Because she is stupid!*' I'd answer myself and smile.

Lost in my thoughts, I grabbed the water bottle from the table. I filled my mouth with fluid, glancing at Amma now and then and decided to focus on Amma again. While I was twisting the lid to seal the blue plastic bottle, Amma said,

"Dhup se thodi hue hain mere baal safed." The most awaited punchline of all times. This translated to *'Afterall sunlight hasn't turned my hair grey'*. That was actually quite funny if you think about it. I mean, whose hair turns grey or white due to the rays of the sun. I shrieked into laughter, trying hard to swallow the water in my mouth. I found that one liner so hilarious that I ended up laughing and choking at the same time and all the water squirted over my mothers' light green salwar suit.

"Peeth pe maro! Peeth pe..!", Amma said. She meant *pat her back.*

My mother who was boiling with anger, couldn't restrain herself from slapping me across the face before smacking my back violently to revive me from the deadly situation. I coughed, laughed, choked again and again. I was breathing heavily and under my sternum, I could feel an ache. Mother kept rubbing my back until I resolved my composure.

I sighed heavily. "I am going to kill you myself, if you do that again!", my mother cursed me. She was all red with anger and was staring me at with her big eyes, which were ready to pop out of their sockets. The slap made me look down in embarrassment.

"Shut up Suman! Don't say such things for kids." I heard Amma reprimand my mother. I moved my head towards the left to see her rugged mountain like face. It was graced with worry. Her white hair reminded me of the punch line. I looked down quickly, as I was about to burst into another round of laughter. I bit my lower lip, trying hard to control. I felt my face getting hotter and butterflies were whizzing inside my stomach. I closed my eyes, trying not to think about the punchline and focused on Amma and mother.

"This girl Amma…when will she grow!", my mother asked in despair.

"Kids are this way, Suman. It's okay!", Amma replied calmly.

"She's already 21, Amma…"

"She will understand soon, Suman, give her some time."

I opened my eyes, as the situation seemed to be under control now.

"Are you going to complain all night or will you give me something to eat as well?", Amma asked enthusiastically.

"Oh! I've already prepared the dinner Amma. Please come.", mother replied heartily.

"Change your clothes first."

"Yes…yes Amma." Mother took out another pair of salwar suit from the almirah and gave me a deadly look as she went to change. Meanwhile, no conversation took place between Amma and I, with an awkward silence engulfing the room. I stretched my arm to grasp my phone from the table towards the left. Amma was glancing at the phone like a kid while I made myself busy, swiping time and again over the screen of the gadget.

***

"You're going with Amma.", mother told me the next morning.

"Where?"

"Mangla", she answered.

"What? No! I am not going certainly. No Maa, I won't go."

"Why? Why won't you go?", mother interrogated, raising an eyebrow.

Because Amma knows nothing. She knows nothing about the gizmos that I use. She barely knows about literature. She doesn't know about anything. She hasn't even been to school ever. She's illiterate. She's so dumb! Who will I talk to? With whom will I discuss Amma's rugged mountain like appearance? To whom will I tell Amma's silly punchlines and laugh with? Amma, herself? No...never! She cries over the pettiest of things! I don't want to waste my precious vacation listening to stupid tales from a stupid old woman...

"I have other plans Maa...", I replied. Though hundreds of thoughts were running inside my head at that time, I told my mother only this. If I had divulged the actually reason, mother would have not wasted a single second to land her leather chappal over my face.

"What plans?", she raised her eyebrows.

"Plans! Ummm... I have plans, Maa." *Plans like I have to meet all my school friends, whom I haven't seen since long. I have to boast about my college in Delhi and make them envious. I have to visit the new lovers point in the town, so that someday I can visit there with Rahul...*

"Come on, say something Aashi!", she interrupted my unending thoughts.

"Rahul….", I replied absent mindedly.

"Rahul, who Rahul?", she asked in confusion.

"Rahul! My schoolmate, Maa…" *what if Maa came to know about me and Rahul? Oh no! She's staring at me…*

I looked away as the sudden rush of blood across my cheeks made them red. I realized that I was already blushing.

Okay Aashi, cool…cool. You have to act normal.

"Remember, short height-spiky hair?" She nodded thoughtfully.

"Yeah, so….I have to meet, Maa….meet Rahul's…."

"Rahul's mom!" *yes, a perfect excuse.*

"Yes…Oh…Maa. I have to finish my story. You remember I was writing a story?" *Thank god, I had a valid reason!*

"You've been writing it since last year, and you're still not able to complete it. I don't think you will."

"I couldn't finish because I haven't found the right inspiration and muse to do justice to my story yet. I need to talk to people, know their experiences and stories.", I interrupted my mother to defend myself.

"What was the theme?", she enquired.

"Women are warriors", I lied, unsure of the repercussions.

"Then, you should definitely go with Amma!", she exclaimed with excitement.

"No!" *I shouldn't have told her the theme.* I regretted my choice of words.

"See, your Baba and I are going to Kangra to meet Chauhan Uncle. He's suffering from cancer. It's urgent." She looked serious. *Vikram uncle has cancer? How? Why didn't you tell me this earlier Maa?* I thought. His jolly face flashed in front of my eyes. It was sad to know about his ailment. The news made me forget about Amma and Rahul for a while.

"We can't leave you alone here. Go with Amma for a week. We'll be back soon.", she convinced me so politely that I couldn't deny. Moreover, their meeting with Vikram Uncle was more important than my meeting with Rahul.

"Okay Maa, I'll go..." I felt heavy. *I can handle Amma for a week, right?!* I thought.

Mother kissed me on the forehead. "Good girl", she said softly. I smiled too.

*****

Welcome to Mangla, Aashi!

I made a tighter grip across the slings of my back pack and stepped out of the taxi. I looked for Amma and saw that she was still seated in the cab, rummaging inside her black leather purse for money.

"How much, *beta*?", she asked for the fare.

"400 rupees, Aunty ji.", he said.

"400 is a lot, *bhaiya*, we'll give only 200." I tried to apply my bargaining skills which I'd learnt in Delhi. They'll loot you, you know; if you'll not.

"No *Didi*, it's fixed."

'This guy is saying four hundred rupees! I mean seriously?! No, I am not going to pay him a penny more than 200 rupees' I thought.

"No. We'll pay 200 hundred only.", I folded my arms and stared at him.

Wait, Why wasn't Amma saying anything? Why wasn't she taking my side?

I glanced at her for support. But she was busy in arranging rupees ten, fifty and hundred rupees notes, still sitting inside the cab.

Ugh...say something Amma! Come on!

She didn't. She was as calm and as the Pir Panjals.

Huh, never mind. I decided to sort it by myself.

"Last time *bhaiya*, we'll not...."

"Eighty... ninety... hundred. Here, four hundred. Take this son." Amma paid the fare. I was snubbed. I mean she paid the entire fare, without even showing some disdain towards the amount. She slid her hips over the seat and shifted herself towards the left door and came out from the car, adjusting her gnarled hands over her arthritic knees.

She crossed the road towards the right and I followed; thinking all the time that Amma was so dumb.

There was a confectionary shop where Amma entered to buy some stuffs. The middle-aged woman, who was probably the owner of the shop, asked Amma about me. She passed a smile and I faked it too. Amma was done with shopping and we headed towards her house. It was about half a kilometer away. Pretty near, right? We trekked uphill to cover this half kilometer! *Two minutes silence for my highly adventurous start to a super amazing vacation (sarcasm intended).*

***

"Why do you cry so much, Amma?", I asked her after we had finished lunch.

She glanced at me and smiled. Her eyes were looking like an ocean in a storm. Her pupil had become milky due to cataract. It appeared like the foam over the ocean, holding immense secrets.

"Tell na, Amma!", I appealed to her.

"Life has not been a bed of roses for me, dear Aashi. It has rather been a path of thorns. You are a lucky girl." Tears reappeared in her eyes. She wiped them and continued-

"We were five sisters and I was the youngest. My parents were famers. They never sent us to school as in those times, people used to think that educating girls would bring disaster.", she rambled on.

"So the only thing we were taught was domestic work. I got married when I was 15 years old."

"15 years?", I responded, as this piqued my interest.

I am 21 and I still think I am a kid and Amma got married when she was 15!

"I menstruated for the first time in my *Sasural (in laws' house)*. It might sound stupid. But yes, girls used to get married early. Your Dada (grandfather) was in the police. He used to call me Radha.", she blushed at the mention of my grandfather, just like a teenager in love. Her smile was somewhat a mixture of joy and sorrow.

"Within a year, I became pregnant with your father inside my womb. Your *Bua* (aunt) is three years younger than Rinku (my father). Everything was going well. We were happy. Your Dada would often take us to certain places and melas (fairs) and buy us anything we wanted. Then suddenly, everything ended like a beautiful dream" Her expressions changed. Her lips drooped down again, like a wilted leaf.

"It was midnight. Your Dada was out for his night duty. Reema(aunt), Rinku and I were sleeping quite peacefully. Suddenly, somebody knocked the door. I walked towards the door, rubbing my sleepy eyes, thinking that it was your Dada."

"Who was at the door, Amma? Was it Dada?", I asked out of curiosity.

"There were four people and your Dada. He was dead.", she broke down.

I wanted to console Amma at that time. I felt sorry for her loss. Though, I didn't say anything.

"They told me that he had met with an accident. And that incident was the turning point of my life. Everything just turned around in the blink of an eye. All the happy dreams that your Dada and I had build over the years, gone in an instant. I, a 19 year old girl was left alone with two kids. Rinku was 3 years old and Reema, she was only six months old.

Jeth ji (brother in law) kicked us out of the house after a year. 'What was my fault?' I'd think and weep. I shifted to the *Guwad* (barn) which was in the backyard of the house. The backyard was linked to the main street of the village. I remember, people used to mask their nose with some cloth whenever my kids would go to greet them."

"Why?", I couldn't understand.

"To avoid the smell of cow dung. They'd often shoe away Rinku and Reema."

Eww…but still, people shouldn't have behaved like this. I shook my head in disapproval.

"Amma, me too. I cannot withstand its smell for even 5 seconds…"

"Imagine, my kids have lived there for 5 years!" I was snubbed again.

"After some time, I got your Dada's pension. Twenty rupees was a large amount then. I used that money to buy groceries, to pay school fees of the kids. In the evening, when Rinku and Reema would fall asleep, I used to ask God *'what kind of justice is this God? Why me?'* I would get no answer…"

Amma paused. She was already crying like a child. Tears were oozing out of her eyes and her nose was running. She rubbed her palms against her eyes to make her vision clearer and, took a corner of her blue- green checked *Kameez* to wipe her nose.

I wanted to laugh, but that day, I didn't as I saw Amma in a different light. And in those tears, I saw frustration, anguish and hopelessness.

"When did you shift to Mangla then, Amma?", I tried to continue the conversation. She sighed.

"We were forced to leave. My *Guwad* collapsed. I requested *Jeth ji* for shelter, but he and his wife denied. I had no expectations with *Jeth ji* , but I had some hopes from his wife.

"You know why?", she asked me.

"Why Amma?" I had no clue.

"Because she was my own sister, dear Aashi!", her voice choked, and I was shocked. Shocked to discover how her own sister betrayed and shunned her away during tough times.

"Once, I asked her to lend me some money to pay Rinku's school fees as I could not save money that month. She obviously refused. *'It'd be better if you employ him at some Dhaba to wash utensils. Your lanky chap ain't going to be some Collector and all…'* *Didi* (sister) said. Her comment ached me more than her denial for lending money.

'I'll send them to school even if I have to sell myself in the market.' I replied. This incident left me shattered that my own sister refused to help me but this made me more self reliant. I sold my silver chain which your Dada had gifted me, to pay the fees.

When this wasn't enough, I was denied rights over our house and our land too. My kids were being tortured continuously and my pension money was often snatched. After tolerating all this for 5 years, I finally decided to come here, where my mother resided. She had known everything and hence, she accepted us."

Amma's backstory had put me in a pandemonium. Never had I ever imagined a saga filled with pain, betrayal, anguish behind her sagged skin. *May be that's why she didn't bargain with the taxi driver. She knew the pain of being denied.* I was trying to draw reasons behind her actions. The more I was curious to know, the more Amma was eager to tell. It appeared as if she had always wanted to tell. She continued to speak and I listened carefully.

"Now, pension money was not at all enough. We used to grow rice and wheat in the fields. I had even worked as a laborer at construction sites. There was a man there, Titu."

Oh, so Amma had some followers too! I got more interested. But my excitement soon faded away when she told,

"He was a drunkard. My mother had always warned me against him as she had noticed him following me all the time. One day, he tried to misbehave even. I don't know from where the courage came but I grabbed a wooden rod from somewhere and taught him a bitter lesson."

"Ouch!", I laughed. I was happy to discover that Amma didn't choose to cry that time. She actually fought. I glanced at her with my eyes and mouth wide open. *So, this cry baby – stupid Amma is so much more strong than she lets on!* I felt proud.

She laughed at me. May be, I was looking stupid at that time.

"I worked all day and night, to make a better future for my kids.", she added.

"Tabhi to buddhe ko dhol mein daala tha!", she mocked. *It says - That's why the old man was put inside the drum!*

"What?", I couldn't understand this one. *Which old man? Did Amma have another admirer?*

"Now, let's go. We're getting late.", she stood and headed towards the room.

 I followed her, seeking answers to all my queries.

"Amma! Which old man? Do you want to say you'd a boyfrie…."

"Shhh…Aashi! Naughty girl!"

"Accha, okay, tell me one thing…"

***

Dear diary,

"God always tries to drown you in the things you hate. Not that he hates you, just to teach you and help you grow."

Sometimes the worst things happen to us only to help us in the long run, we become better prepared for such type of situations in the future. Maybe this was a sign from God. My trip to Mangla with Amma definitely changed my perspective and outlook about a lot of things. In Delhi, I used to miss this view…the mountains, fresh air, fields and peace! Ah! No diary, don't think I don't love Delhi. I love Delhi too. It's just now I value this solitude because somewhere deep inside I have always longed for this serene and peaceful ambience. Absolutely beautiful, a cottage over the hill with nobody around except for Pine trees and many-hued fluttering butterflies. And you know what is the best part? Well, let me tell you. The town of Chamba in its entirety is visible from here and it is quite aesthetic for the mind and soul. Chaos often looks so beautiful, right?!

What! You want to know about Amma? Oh diary, I forgot, I am saawwrryyy! A week has passed by in a jiffy and Maa and Baba didn't come to take me back. They told me, they will come next week as Vikram uncle had passed away. I was upset. Not much upset about Vikram Uncle passing away; more upset because I had to stay with Amma for seven more days .

Anyways, let me tell you, Amma's daily routine. Amma, wakes up at 5:00 in the morning. She freshens up and exactly at 6:00 a.m., she starts reciting Durga Chalisa in front of the idol of the goddess. It serves as a tiny temple in the house. She rings the bell of the temple and chants certain mantras. She doesn't wake me, but her "bhajan kirtan" spoils my sleep. Once my sleep has disappeared, I have no other choice other than to get up. I mean, who wakes up so early, diary? Well, Amma does…hahaa funny. Then she makes some tea for us and serves it with bread or paratha and biscuits often.

She'd then goes to unwind the leashes on Laali and Bhuri. These two are so cute. I often offer them straws of grass which they accept happily. Laali rotates her head in gratitude while Bhuri licks my hands with her rough tongue. Animals too have human instincts. Amma takes them to the backyard and ties them to a pole in the sunlight. Bhuri resists to be tied which makes Amma curse her after which she quietly stands there like an innocent child. Amma always ties Laali first because, she loves her sister Bhuri so much that once , while Amma was cursing Bhuri like any other day, Laali came to defend Bhuri. She was about to hit Amma and fire her like a rocket in air. Thank god, Amma was saved that day. Otherwise, that would become another reason for the damn waterworks to start.

Amma serves her giant pets with grass and places buckets of water infront of each of them. Then, she'd clean the Guwad (bedroom of Laali and Bhuri) and throw gobar(cow dung) on the heap outside the Guwad. She'd clean and curse simultaneously...and it's too funny too see her quick actions. I wish I had learned Pahadi as well, so that I could understand her funny dialogues more. But it's no harm, I can manage with Hindi.

I also help her in the domestic work. Like, I clean the room and wash utensils often.....and...sing ....and eat...and sleep and....oh diary! Do you want me to feel guilty that I am lazy? I wonder how Amma manages to do all the work by herself.

By the time all our tasks done, it is afternoon and she cooks some meal for us. We rest for some time. In the evening, Amma goes to the backyard to tie Laali and Bhuri back in the Guwad while I sit in the verandah and watch the peaceful view of the chaotic Chamba town. And now, Amma has gone to prepare dinner. Yeah, people in villages, eat early and sleep early. You know 'early to bed, early to rise' phrase!

Twilight is approaching and I am still mesmerized by the beauty of the place. The lights over the mountains twinkle like stars and it looks so adorable. The breeze gives me the chills and I love it. I often take deep breaths so that my lungs can accommodate as much air as they can. The view so crystal clear....

You know another surprising thing that happened?! I barely use the phone now. I usually get so busy in observing the scenery that I often forget to call Rahul. Can you imagine? Yesterday, we quarreled over this but it's okay. It happens you know. Amma is not that much stupid . She's a bit cute! I noticed she hasn't cried a single time since that day. Her story is a tragic one. There's a lot to learn - endurance, courage, kindness, love. It's sad how she was betrayed by her own people. I regret that I made her feel embarrassed. I think how stupid I was to think that Amma was stupid. She is genuine when expressing her emotions. She is a hero! She managed to survive and stand all alone and it has smelted her into a strong woman. I admire her strength and courage. I thought I won't be able to find the right inspiration for my story. But now, I have a great journey to narrate, which is going to inspire hundreds of lives out there. We, the so-called new generation constantly rushing here and there in search of a speck of inspiration to liven our monotonous lives. Little do we realize how close it resides!

Oops, dinner time. Amma is calling. I'll come later, okay. I love you♡

Yours,

Aashi

LAKSHMI NARAYAN

"To write, is to create an art form of thoughts and imaginations which will not happen easily and is rarely favourable to us. To write, is to enjoy the emotions we lack or fail to realise in our reality, all the time." ~ Lakshmi Narayan

A fan of sublime emotions, he is always experimenting with words whenever he sits down to writ. A pinch of ardour in his poems, quotes, stories evokes overwhelming responses from the reader! More inclined to the romance genre but always up for experimenting other genres as well!

Follow him on Instagram - @_narayan

It was definitely not a good night. My heart embellished with darkness. Art and the artists should always be prepared for rejections and I was definitely not. In that rejected phase, I went through a quick slideshow of my past.

My childhood was filled with random colours and radiant visuals. Canvases, sheets of paper, pencils and colours – that was it to break the monotony of my life even when I was a child. All I thought back then was if I could make the world my canvas, paint all the beautiful things present in this world and give the world a different perspective altogether.

Growing up, from a child with pencils to a teenager with brushes was a massive change which was definitely incredible. Every single time, I used to hold the brush in my hand, the only thought that ran through my mind was the different kinds of artistic expressions a painter can present with a mere brush and a canvas. Being occupied by sheets of paper and brushes was not a problem for me as I was kind of a wallflower who didn't interact much, no friends and girlfriends, was something I did not experience because of my mundane personality. Years went by in solitude during my school and college years and I didn't mind that at all. These days, many people post memes about going back to their childhood phase and that is something I could relate to as I too didn't like to be an adult. But that was not happening anytime soon so, I looked ahead and saw the path of adulthood. I was not ready but I couldn't escape this phase.

Being an adult was not very hard for me, as I was not into adulting like my colleagues. I had shunned away social media too at one point of time but I decided against it. As I had social media accounts, I decided to do something out of the ordinary by posting my portraits and depictions. Yeah, that would be too much even for me, I thought. But, I wanted to be noticed even if it was by a small number of people. That's, when I began to post my paintings with a single hashtag that would describe that painting but that didn't suffice in a good outcome. The sense of rejection had already seeped in and I started to believe that my paintings were not good enough. I didn't post anything for a while. I felt like I was going through a breakup, ironically, I had never experienced one. What hurt me more was the fact that I didn't know what needed to be improved.

Then, I found out that my painting didn't depict any human emotions. I began to understand that anything which reflects human emotions is boom, viral content. So, I brought various emotions into my paintings. I wanted to bring them to life so that people wouldn't scroll away, without at least glancing at my post for 2 seconds. I painted all day and all night. But that time, I didn't paint just to get noticed. I painted them so that I could live in those different emotions. I took all the untold emotions in my life and splattered it into my paintings. I painted my worries, my heart breaks and my disappointments with the world. Most of my paintings reflected the miseries of people. I started to get responses. What would be a better thing for an artist than a driving and an unstoppable motivation.

After college got over, most of my friends (yes, I made friends, another big change) took jobs from MNCs and some went abroad for their masters. I didn't want to do either of that. I just wanted to live with whatever I could have by doing what I love. I wanted a break from all those free advices and annoying suggestions made by my family, relatives and friends.

I decided to take a trip to beautiful places nearby and so, I went to Munnar. Oh man! What a place that was. I could see why it's a famous place for honeymoon or even a simple vacation. That place was just lovely and even people who aren't in a relationship, will fall in love with nature's ravishing looks. I couldn't leave that place. I wanted to live at least a part of my life there. I returned after a week, that too reluctantly and started painting again. One of my friends called me the day I was back and we talked about many useless things for a long duration. Just as we were about to hang up on each other, he told me about an art exhibition that was going to happen next month and asked me to participate. I never thought of displaying my paintings in an exhibition as I was not sure whether my paintings were good enough for an art exhibition. I googled "how to prepare for an art exhibition" and learned some new ways to project what was necessary.

I then contacted the exhibition team and asked whether they could display my paintings there. They gave me an appointment with their manager and asked me to bring my best paintings there.

I had prepared myself and went to the said address to meet the manager. I was very excited to get my paintings out of social media into the real world. I went inside the hall and waited there. A tall sturdy man walked towards me, with a smile. That man had all the looks of a manager. He asked about my qualifications and my experiences with art. When I showed my paintings to him, he didn't even react a bit. He looked at them like a professor would look at exam papers.

That worried me a little. After looking through some of my paintings, he gave a sigh and said that my paintings were not professional and added that many of them expressed the saddest sides of life and that would not be a positive display for an art exhibition. This downside had hammered me down terribly.

I said "thank you" and walked out of that place, with no emotion whatsoever gracing my face so as to not display the inner turmoil going through me. I couldn't walk any further as I lost every inch of the façade that I had put up in front of the manager. I sat on a roadside bench and stared at my paintings. I couldn't stop thinking about what he said. Although he didn't say that my paintings were bad, he mentioned that those were not professional. I knew that I was not a professional painter but still I couldn't just accept that rejection. I kept staring at my paintings. That's when I noticed a sheet of paper lying right next to my shoes. Though I was not in the mood to read anything at the moment, I couldn't just throw that away. There was a poem written in that paper.

"the girl with the red flower holding the pain
she cannot die again and even if she did, that
might go in vain
following the traces that leads her far away
she could not end her journey in that rainy day"

I couldn't understand exactly what that poem was about but I could sense a pain and pain was what makes us remember our purpose in life. I felt an urge to read it to its entirety. After reading the poem in that paper, I felt a need to read more poems. As I haven't read much poems in my life, expressing pain through words felt very different to me although so very beautiful. So, I searched for a name in that paper. Ah! There was a name "Aarohi" written at the bottom. I took my mobile next second and started searching for that poet. There were many accounts with the name Aarohi. I looked into all those accounts and finally found her. The name was "aarohi_writings". I shouted, "Yesss" that's when I realised that I hadn't gone home yet. I booked a cab and left for home. I couldn't wait to read those poems. There were 105 posts in that account and the one I had read had been uploaded a month ago. I read nearly 50 poems and was in awe by how the emotions were expressed with beautiful words. I was a fan of her work. I didn't want to miss any of her poems. I clicked the follow button and said good night to her poems and my paintings.

Next morning, I woke up to check if she had posted anything but surprisingly, she hadn't. That disappointed me a little. I kept on checking her account every minute I got but nothing, zilch. I felt kind of empty. I didn't know whether that's because I got rejected or the girl, who was a complete stranger to me, hadn't posted any of her poems. I didn't want to skip painting. So I stood up to start painting. But I couldn't think of any ideas. I didn't want to paint any random thing for the sake of colouring my canvas. I kept on thinking and that's when I saw her poem. I thought that wouldn't it be beautiful if her words were portrayed as emotions with colors on my canvas. After painting as best as I could, I felt like my painting had gotten a new form. I took a picture and posted it on Instagram.

I started my day with the comments on my last post. One of the comments gave me a shock. Someone had commented "Brother, why did you post this again?". On reading that particular comment, questions like "When did I paint this? Was he testing me? Was he joking or something?" flooded my mind. I scrolled down the feed and was shocked to see that I did already paint a very similar one that showed a girl longing to die while living. I used roses that were covered with blood and the girl holding them running towards death.

I couldn't believe that my painting was exactly described as a poem. I got suffocated with too many questions. I, then decided to consider that as a strange coincidence and that's when I saw the date on the post. That's exactly a month ago. I remembered that Aarohi had posted that poem a month ago with the caption "roses and blood".

I was freaking out, no kidding. I, then began to check her poetries with my paintings. She posted her poetries exactly at the same date on which I had posted my paintings. Each and every one of her poetries' dates and descriptions matched with mine. That's not some coincidence or any trick, right?! I checked them once again to reassure myself.

In one of my paintings, there's a man who has cut his heart out, with a grin lacing his face. I checked her poetry that she had written on the same date.

"Smile all the way, man
Love is not a game to plan
Cut your heart out and throw it over
Life is not to live forever"

In another painting, where I had painted a girl cutting her wings off her back, Aarohi had written

"Screw the freedom girl
You're not here to whirl
Why have wings on your back
When you don't even fight back"

I felt like reading my paintings. I read all her poems and they matched exactly. But she was not following my page. She might be secretly following me and my paintings. But, she didn't post her poem yesterday. I wondered what might have happened last night. After giving it a lot of thought, I texted her. I wanted to know about her. So I checked her followings list. I was surprised to see that she had been following only one person, who went by the name, Ananya. I thought she must be her only best friend and I might get to know something if I talked to her. So I texted her too.

Both of them didn't text back and I couldn't stop checking my mobile. Ananya posted a story on that day. It was a picture and it shocked me to the core. She had written "Get well soon, Aarohi!", with a picture of a girl lying on a hospital bed with injuries on her head and legs. I felt heartbroken in that very second.

She didn't feel like a stranger anymore. She admired my paintings and gave life to them through beautiful words. Questions like 'What if she was in love with me and what if I was falling for her too?' troubled me. I hadn't seen her or even met her but I couldn't just say she was a stranger anymore. I flashed back into reality when I heard a notification sound. I expected a simple 'hey!' but the first message she sent was "how did you find out?" I told her the events of yesterday and asked her, "What happened to Aarohi?". She told me, "It would be better if we could talk about this in person!" I said, "Okay!" and asked her the hospital address.

That hospital was just 30 minutes away from my place. I rushed to see the girl who had consumed my mind and wanted to know more about her and the connection of her poetry to my paintings. I saw Ananya waiting at the hospital entrance. I jogged towards us and enquired about Aarohi.

She said, "Aarohi is my childhood friend. She was a single child and became an orphan just 2 years back. Depression and panic attacks had engulfed her life since the death of her parents. She shunned away everything that she loved, college, writing. But 5 months later, Aarohi came back to college, looking better and less grief-stricken. On asking her, she showed me a painting of yours, where you had painted a little girl who had been standing alone with a picture of her mom and dad. She told me that painting resembled her and she didn't want to stand alone like that little girl. After that, your paintings became our lunchtime conversations. She admired your work and started writing poems that would describe your paintings. Your paintings had become her company, her friend. She fell in love with your paintings. Along the way, she had also developed feelings for you. She wanted to be with you and your paintings. But she didn't want you to know that. She wanted to meet you personally and express her feelings towards you and your paintings. She saw your Instagram story on that day and worked up the courage to go to the museum just to meet you. She asked me to get a printed copy of her poems and bring them there.

While I was nearing the museum, I got a phone call that Aarohi had met with an accident and she had been taken to the nearby hospital. I left in a hurry without even informing you about anything. But see, fate works in a strange way. She met with an accident and you got rejected. The poem that was in my file unexpectedly reached you and now you're here".

I was shell-shocked after listening to Ananya. I ran to Aarohi's room and stood beside her bed, admiring her beauty and innocence, even though she was connected to multiple tubes and was maimed badly. The hands that grazed paper after paper to give out the most beautiful poems best suited for my paintings, was resting there and I couldn't hold myself from touching her hands and caressing them. In that moment, everything was forgotten and was a blur. All that mattered was Aarohi. When I heard the door close, I knew it was Ananya who would've wanted to check up on Aarohi. The doctors came for their periodic checkup and told us to hold on and support her.

But I had something else going on in my mind. I didn't want to meet Aarohi with empty hands. So, I did what I do best – paint. I wanted to give to Aarohi the moments which she had dreamt of on the day she was on her way to meet me. After painting that beautiful, intimate moment of ours from that day, I named it as 'Our Place In The Painting'.

SAI TANISHQ

"Writing can be impactful if you just trigger a thought, keep that thought into practice and bring a change." ~ **Sai Tanishq**

An optimist who creates an ambience in the field of writing by connecting dots differently which enables readers to have an engaging experience. Suspense, Thriller, Mystery, whatever the genre be, trust him to bring out the avant-garde version through his style of writing. Considering the witty tone of his plotlines, you will always be in for a surprise.

Follow him on Instagram - @thecreativeshelf

29 NOVEMBER 2017, 7:30 A.M, ARJUN'S HOME...

Just like every morning, a beam from the rising red sun penetrated through the double door of the brownish tinted window, which was on the first floor of a single-storey building. They tried hard to wake up Arjun as much as I did (*No time for introductions because Arjun was late again*). Mom might have pushed away the blue coloured, silk curtains, early this morning in order to wake Arjun up.

"Time to get some energy", she said in a monotonous tone.

"Yeah, probably he's only left with a few kilocalories of energy in his body", I replied analyzing the energy levels. Arjun had an irritated face. All of a sudden, he removed the black, woolen quilt which had kept him warm last night.

"Don't you ever wake me up without the mention of food?", Arjun whined as he gently rubbed his eyes.

"That's what gives us energy, even to get irritated you know?" I tried explaining to him as I did most of the time. "Shut the ....", Arjun broke in between and said, "I want to start my day pleasantly."

I knew what he was going to say and as a matter of fact, I didn't want to hear them either, this early.

"Anyways, it's time! Gear up!", I reminded him.

"Instant energy is needed", she explained to me. "That's right, we're running out of time! Eggs and banana will do the job", I replied.

"Arjun, it's better to tell mom that you will eat a boiled egg or an omelette.", I continued.

"Maa...", he yelled while he washed his fair face after brushing his teeth and continued to say, "I will have an omelette and a banana today. Nothing else!" Mom did hear it with extra bass as he was in the bathroom.

"You should have some milk too, okay?", Mom replied.

"That will be even better", she quickly responded.

"You never want to waste an opportunity, right?", I told her. "It's already 7:45 a.m, Arjun. We'll see if we do have a few minutes in our hand to grab that glass of milk.", I said in a hurry. Arjun didn't respond to mom's comment. He hurriedly completed his bath before the bucket filled, with the tap running.

"Ahh...what to choose?", he asked himself for a second or two, surfing amongst the ocean of shirts he had (at least he felt that way). "Choose the black one", I said.

"What ?... Maa would kill me!", he reacted. After a lot of deliberation, he had no option but to pick that shirt as it was the only ironed one in his wardrobe and it looked elegant on his fit and fair-skinned physique. He dressed as if the mirror vanished the next second.

"I don't need your suggestions now because I'm wearing this one. Maa would ask me to undress the very next second if I don't wear this in contrast with the black shirt.", Arjun said, without a beat as he wanted me to shut up while he wore his cream coloured cotton pants and tightened the black leather belt. He combed back his bulky, black hair looking at his mirror image. "This little pimple on my nose is pissing me off!", he spoke to himself.

"Arjun, you'll get more pissed if you get late anymore! Look at the time!", I warned him, indicating towards the clock, which just ticked 8:05 a.m. "Arjun! Socks, to your right, on the table!", I reminded him before he headed to the kitchen.

"Pick it up, fold it and put it in the mouth in one go", I said pointing the omlette. "Grab the banana", I said as he started running with the backpack.

"Why this black shirt now? Such a lazy kid you are! You sleep late, you wake up late and then you don't even eat properly either.", mom grumbled, caring about her son's malnourished state. Arjun didn't respond as there was no time to strike up an argument over trivial matters. He knew why he was awake till late last night.

'8:10 am' He checked his digital, leather wristwatch while he tied the last knot of his black and white coloured casual shoes.

8:12 A.M, THE CHASE...

"Enough! We have some time, don't we?! So where are we running in a hurry?", she asked. Most of the time, though her instinct worked, she doesn't know the reason why it worked. Neither Arjun did. I thought to make him know tonight, for a purpose. I didn't respond to her, there wasn't any time for that. (*Also, for any intros*)

'8:15 am' the wristwatch on his left hand showed.

"It's over, I guess. You are late already.", I told Arjun.

"You are 500 meters away and less than 3 minutes are left.", I continued to say. He slowed down a bit. His breathing pace was faster than his foot pace. His mouth was open, wanting more oxygen into his lungs. But I sensed, something triggered Arjun to not stop at all.

"Even in the worst cases of you winning, never stop fighting" mom's phrases lingering at the back of his mind. He closed his mouth. He closed his eyes, still running at a slow pace. Suddenly he took all the air he could, in a single pull with his nose. "It isn't done yet", he said and started running with an energy, more than a glass of glucose could do justice.

He saw it. There wasn't much distance left. He continued to run faster. "Arjun caref...", I prompted, unfinished as he stepped up on to the first step of his college bus in the blink of an eye. He ascended the other three steps and got into a vacant seat. His wristwatch ticked '8:18 a.m'.

"Calm down Arjun, close your mouth, inhale through your nose and exhale through your mouth.", I told him. After a minute, he settled down, breathing quite normally.

"Quickest one, right?", he asked me.

"Yes! Though you aren't playing football anymore, the basics have helped you in the long run.", I praised him. "All thanks to Coach!", he smiled and responded.

But more than his soccer fitness basics, what drove him at that very instant was something mom had taught him. Mom used to always motivate him by telling him inspiring stories before his sleep till he was 14. I always wondered how mothers create such an impact, striking at the right time even if it were small hurdles.

Once, it's luck. Twice, it's strength. Thrice, it's a blessing! Moms are magical! Their skills & superpowers are far better than a psychiatrist's and even more so inspiring than a motivational speaker's.

"Hey! Brother, won't you ever try to be on time?", inquired Suhas. Suhas was his bus companion for the past 2 years. He was Arjun's junior, studying at the same college.

"I don't know, buddy. Maybe, I'm too calculative.", Arjun replied.

"Give me some time, we'll get back later", he continued to say while opening his book and glancing at his notes. It was all his short-notes, keywords and mind maps that he created for himself to minimize the study time.

"Arjun, leave your mind fresh and pleasant.", I advised.

 "True. Better.", He comprehended.

"Where are we heading to?", she raised a question again.

"There's still time for you. Why do you intervene? Arjun's going to college. He has his physiology exam today", I responded, trying to be as brief as possible.

"Bye, buddy. Let's meet again.", Arjun waved his right hand at Suhas.

"Bye brother.", Suhas waved back with a smile.

9:05 A.M, ARJUN'S COLLEGE...

"I believe, I have prepared well, right?!", Arjun said walking towards the examination hall. The silhouettes of the elevated, brick designed pillars fell on him as he continued to walk.

"You haven't", I said.

"What? What did I forget?", Arjun screamed out in fear.

"Chill out. I'm just kidding.", I joked.

"Idiot, you are! You'll end up pissing me off every time!", he cried out in anger.

He was about to get into the room when he noticed the red, digital clock above the room's entrance which indicated '9:10 a.m'. He took out his hall ticket from the left shirt pocket with his right hand and checked it, confirming the exam details.

"Physiology, 9:30 a.m,
room number 7,
3, 6C." it was mentioned.

Arjun got seated in the place allotted to him. Third row, sixth chair. A light brownish plank was attached to the iron chair which was painted in black. The room would be seating 24 more students for this examination. Arjun was elated to see a white coloured fan right above him that had broad wings, which meant that he didn't have to feel uncomfortable due to perspiration during the exam. The walls were painted in a typical white colour (colours like that for a college classroom didn't last that long) with a green board and a wooden table in the front.

A female invigilator entered the room with paper piles.

"Is she a strict one?", he asked himself.

"Usually, I talk less and work more. I do the same here. I only do my signature writing malpractice if I find any issue", the invigilator cleared everyone's doubts with a single, blunt response.

"Though every invigilator says this, she looks strict enough. I just don't want to get caught for something I don't even do.", he explained to himself. She walked to each chair distributing the question paper and the answer sheets, one by one. Arjun's pulse had quickened as she approached him. He received the question paper and answer sheet. Without wasting anymore time, he started to go through the question paper. "Seems okay. Not really tough", he spoke to himself. He began writing the answers. His mind maps flowed into words on to the sheet with the blue and black combination pens. His happiness for the fan didn't last very long as the excessive fluttering of the papers annoyed him. He managed to stop the fluttering with the stationery he had and continued to write. He was drawing diagrams and humming his favourite song simultaneously, in a low volume.

"Damn, these diagrams. They consume a lot of time.", Arjun got irked. He then noticed the invigilator standing beside him with a red ink pen. At that very instant, the eraser fell from his hands.

"What nonsense are you doing in an exam hall?", she questioned, gravely with an eye brow raised.

"Sorry mam", he apologized. He was lucky that she didn't bother him after that.

"Who would concentrate only on writing for three long hours?", he thought. He finished writing the answers. His wristwatch showed '12:05 pm'.

"Psssttt..." Arjun heard something. He looked around and found nothing. He started to recheck his answers.

"Hey..!", a female voice came from the left, just behind him. He turned back, staying alert about the invigilator.

"Hey! Show me the 4th answer.", a girl murmured, asking Arjun. He nodded sideways gesturing he doesn't know that.

"Girls have turned out to be courageous these days!", he thought.

"But when a girl asks you answers during an exam and you don't tell them intentionally, the level of satisfaction you get is high. Especially, when you live in a society where people think most girls study well", he continued to think. After scrutinizing his answer sheet, Arjun got up, handed over his answer sheet and walked out from the left exit of the room. He took his backpack from the other room where all the bags were kept and headed towards the college bus. He sighed in relief. His face was bright with a smile gracing his face. It was his last exam. End of the academic year in his college.

"Vacation begins. Yes!" He was in joy.

"You aren't a kid anymore, Arjun. It's stupid that even at the age of 22 you are going high for the holidays.", I said to him.

"The meaning of holidays does not change with age. You don't know shit. Shut up", he replied.

"Something chilled would be better.", she said. "He just came out and you started again. But yeah, it's a 40-minutes journey back home.", I got convinced. Arjun was waiting near the bus and it would soon get filled with other students. The canteen was opposite the bus.

"Quite a sunny day, right? How about some juice?", he asked me.

"Weather these days is quite unpredictable.", I replied. He walked towards the canteen.

"What should I order?", He asked, looking at the menu.

"Orange juice is good here, right?", I counter asked him. "Okay, orange juice it is.", he nodded. He took the orange juice and found the bus getting filled enough to start.

"Not again, Arjun. I can't!", I told him.

"I'm not going to run either. Keep calm", he countered.

"You always want to mute me. Am I a joke to you?", I questioned him. "Who knows!", he replied smiling as he stepped into the bus and got into his seat.

"So what plans, Arjun? From tomorrow?", I inquired. He pulled out his smartphone from his bag. "Nothing why..." A Whatsapp message popped on the screen instantly when he turned on the internet and he completely forgot to respond to me. He tapped on the message which showed

"Today at 7 pm?"

He read it, grinning widely and told me,

"Not tomorrow, plans start from today!"

"Good amount of spice would be great na", she said. "What? Spice? But why?", I asked perplexed. "Ah! Damn. She doesn't know the reason", I continued. I kept thinking for some time.

"Mmm… yeah! I got that", I found out myself. "So how are we going?", I was about to ask him but he fell into a short nap, his head leaning against the window.

"Window seats are always hypnotic", I thought.

(Won't we ever get any moment to make some self-intoductions?)

1:25 PM, ARJUN'S HOME...

"Maa... I'm home! I'm hungry. Is my special ready?", Arjun called out the next second he opened the door of his house.

"Yes. Almost. How was your exam?", Mom asked.

"Tell the truth", I said.

"Worst ma! Very tough. Just pass maybe", he told Mom.

"Oh! My son always does great things like this", mom praised him. Mom knew that he joked. Both of them smiled.

"Go, go. Freshen up and come back. Delicious dishes are waiting for you", mom excitedly responded.

Arjun washed his face, hands, and legs. He changed his dress to his favourite comfy wear black tracks and the infamous grey tshirt. He wasn't confused about what to wear. Hunger took over clothing choices any time of the day.

Mom waited at the dining table to serve food. He sat and started to eat his favorite chicken biryani.

"How is it?", mom asked.

"Not that good. Ok ok, kinda stuff.", Arjun teased her. Mom smiled with her one eyebrow raised.

"Mom, I'm going out this evening."

"Where?", Mom questioned in surprise.

"Well, let it be a surprise for you till I tell you.", Arjun's eyes lightened.

"Don't want to waste any day of your vacation. Hmm? Okay then, we will talk at night after you come home.", mom said. Arjun's stomach distended. The blue fringed, analog wall clock opposite to where Arjun was seated, showed '2:15 pm'. He thought that he should continue to read the novel that he couldn't finish as he had gotten sidetracked due to the exams. But as he lacked sleep since last night, in less than 10 minutes, he had slept off.

(We don't even get a second to ourselves! Sad story)

5:30 PM, ARJUN'S HOME...

"Haa..get late for this, too", I poked Arjun. He woke up in a snap and searched for his phone.

"What's the time", he asked. He picked up the phone which was placed to his left. The phone's screen showed '5:30 p.m'.

"Sick you are! Why would you scare me every time?", Arjun whined.

"Don't exaggerate. It's perfect. Go.", I whined back. He got up, annoyed.

This time, he washed his face with face wash. His bright face glowed even better. Arjun came back to the cupboard. He sighed.

"No confusions, choose what to wear and then open the cupboard', I said.

"Good idea. Lemme think", he said. "Mmm… sky blue cotton shirt and black cotton pants", he chose.

"Right!", I agreed in an appreciative tone. He opened the cupboard, picked them out and dressed up. He sprayed perfume around his body. Combed his hair over and over looking at the mirror. He admired his smart self.

"Enough is enough. Time to go!", I said trying to push him away from that mirror.

"Don't be envious. Okay?", Arjun told me.

"Oh, okay, sir. Sure!", I obeyed him.

Arjun had put on his same casual shoes again. They were his favourite. His wristwatch showed '6:23 p.m'

"Maa... I'm going on the motorbike.", Arjun said. "Go safely. Come early. You know about your father, right?", mom replied. "Okay…", he drawled away while putting his helmet.

"Where are we going now?", she asked. "Ahh...To see the result of the spices.", I answered sarcastically.

Arjun's face had lit up. Excitement, confidence and fear, he had them altogether. He was going to meet someone, whom he had last met a year ago. Someone, whom he was bonded with, since 6 years. Someone he counts on each day.

After a 15-minute journey, he reached the destination.

6:41 PM, CLOUD 9 RESTAURANT...

'Cloud 9 Restaurant' The restaurant's name had a cloud above which excited (the star-eyed) emojis made into number nine. It was lit with serial lights. Elegant glass designed elevation was impressive enough to check-in at least once.

"Let's get in and wait there", I said. "Even I thought the same.", he replied in a second walking towards the entrance door. The inner restaurant was in a whole, warm-white lighting with cream and brown furniture theme. Music playing in the background elevated the ambience of the restaurant.

"Arjun! She looks pretty. See there, on your left. She's even staring at you", I nudged him towards the waitress.

"Not that great though.", he ignored. But he went to the same table where that lady stood. He sat on the cushioned chair. He picked up his phone from the right pocket and started a conversation.

"I'm here. Where are you? I'm sitting towards the left corner.", he pinged on Whatsapp.

"I'm just 2 minutes away. I'll come there. Heart-eyed emoji, red heart emoji.", the reply came.

"Ok, blushing emoji, red heart emoji", Arjun texted.

Arjun stared at the entrance for a long time. His wristwatch showed '7:07 pm'. The next second, he lifted his head, a girl in a black top and white jeggings stepped in. Her fair complexion contrasted the single black bangle on her left hand and a black-banded wristwatch on her right. She had long, silky, black hair, half-opened. The little hanging, gold-coated ear-rings shined. Excitement dived deep in her liquid and innocent eyes making them gleam more than the warm-white lights. Her reddish-pink lips were like the extracts of the cherry fruit.

"That's not lipstick, you know? That must be lip gloss", I said to Arjun.

"This is why I ask you to shut up. Did I ask you?", Arjun said.

Anu was her name and she walked towards her Aru (that's what she called Arjun) with a wide smile and twinkling eyes.

"There's nothing to get tensed. You are clear. Do good", I told Arjun. He didn't reply. His eyes transfixed on Anu.

"Hi!" she waved her right hand with a broad smile and eye-brows raised look on her face. At that very moment, her heartbeat was also elevated. Arjun waved back and Anu came and sat opposite to Arjun.

Both were looking at each other, shyly not being able to say a word.

"Arjun, now she is just a table away. Speak up!", I said, wanting Arjun to break the silence.

"How are you, long time, no see?", Anu asked suddenly.

"Her vocals are no less than that of a singer's, Arjun", I was amazed at her sweet voice, better than earlier. I tried to zip my mouth later.

"I'm good. Yeah, quite a gap. 1year, 112 days, 11hours", Arjun responded.

"No stats now, please?", Anu softly said, smiling. She hated statistics.

"I can also tell you the minutes and seconds if you need them.", he smiled with his eye-brows up.

"So, how was this one year?", Anu asked.

"I don't know what makes girls so strong to avoid, talk, text or call their loved ones", Arjun spoke, slightly angry.

"It's not easy, Aru. But that's what we promised each other before I flew to London. I didn't want to sidetrack ourselves from our academics and career goals, wasting time on social media.", Anu explained.

"But you know? Each day, twice at the least, I've been asking the distance to shower some kindness, I've been asking the time to bring me some shine, I've been asking my life to gift me your love. Today, all of them came to me, as one, in the form of you, after one long year.", Arjun's words flowed like a poet. Anu was blushing.

She slowly took Arjun's left hand and held it in her right hand clasping with the thumb.

"Thank you, Aru. Thank you for waiting for me. Thank you for understanding me. Thank you for coming into my life and I'm blessed to have you as the love of the life" tears in Anu's eyes were just touching the tip of her eye-lids.

"Don't make this a 'Thank you' meet!", Arjun said smiling. Both of them broke into little laughs. Their happiness, laughs, and smiles were like drizzles in a drought.

They ordered Chinese hot and spicy vegetarian noodles as Anu was a vegetarian. The chilled soft drinks tasted better with the spice.

"So, you said you'll turn into a vegetarian. When is that happening?", Anu asked with her one eye-brow raised, moving her head vertically to act serious.

"Oh did I? I had a super tasty chicken biryani made by mom this afternoon", Arjun replied.

"You……..", she playfully hit Arjun. "Cool! I'll quit that soon. Don't worry", he smiled. Anu was not certain about Arjun turning into a vegetarian. She once asked him casually in their high school days and he accepted that without a second thought.

Arjun looked at his watch when Anu gave a pat on his wrist. His happiness for her touch didn't last long as it showed '8:30 p.m'.

"It's getting late for you, Anu. Let me drop you home!", Arjun said. Anu didn't speak for a second. "Okay!", she nodded. Anu knew Arjun well in their 6-year relationship and she believed in him. Arjun paid the bill and they walked together out of the restaurant.

"She was beautiful, right?", Arjun asked Anu, about the waitress to whom he paid the bill.

"Okay then, I'll hire a cab", Anu instantly responded..

"I can't match that level of spontaneity.", Arjun shook his head, sideways smiling as he unlocked the bike with the key. Anu giggled and stepped up onto the back seat of the motorcycle. Arjun kick-started their journey.

8:35 PM, THE RIDE...

"Arjun, be you, remember your limits.", I alarmed him.

"I know! Mute for some time.", he said like always.

"Aru, what further plans?", Anu asked.

"To spend a few more moments with you, till your stay", Arjun answered.

"Shhh...I got impressed long back. Why are you still trying?", her little hand gave a little slap oh his shoulder.

"Don't hit me, my lovely devil!", Arjun moved his head in reflex.

"Though it sounds like that, that's my priority this vacation", Arjun continued.

"Okay. Granted! Doctor Arjun!", Anu turned into a goddess fulfilling her devotee's wish. A speed of 50 kilometers per hour turned chilling breeze ice cold. Anu was tremulous.

"When are you going back?", Arjun asked. "After 10 days", Anu replied, hugging him from the back and laid her head on his shoulder. Anu needed some warmth but Arjun's temperature rose. His heart skipped a beat.

"You should alert me before you do such things", he spoke breaking in between his words. "My return?", she smiled. She knew what Arjun actually meant by his words.

"We are nearing your street.", Arjun spoke low.

"You can't ask the time, every single time Arjun. You know it's not easy to meet her again knowing her tight schedule", I tried to console him. He didn't want to leave Anu this early. Anu sat back normally. Arjun stopped the bike just at the beginning of the street. Both of them had a little heart-break. A tree branched wider as if it wanted to give some space for the love birds. Anu got down.

"See you, Arjun.", Anu hid her pain behind a smile. Arjun got down and looked sideways with a hand on the motorbike's handle. Anu saw Arjun's teary eye shining due to the white street lights which were situated behind his back obliquely.

Anu held Arjun's left hand. His warm blood wasn't getting colder yet. Anu came even closer. Arjun was still looking sideways. He didn't want to show his pain and make Anu more saddened. Anu took a step closer to Arjun. She slowly held Arjun's cheeks and moved her head closer. She kissed him on the left cheek and stepped back in a blink. Arjun's raising temperature didn't take much time to shed a tear from his right eye.

"Aru, look at me na! The moments we wished for are not very far. Just a year or two and we will be together forever", Anu tried to move Arjun's head wanting him to face her.

"Bye. Take care. I'll always be there for you.", Arjun broke into tears as he gave her a hug at the spur of the moment. Anu's eyes asked each other whether to get confused or be surprised. He went back the next second. Arjun started his motorbike, looked back giving a gentle and genuine smile. He headed to his home. Anu took a left to her home, walking and looking at the giant tree and wiped her tears. She felt heavy. Heavy like never before.

"Take a bow! For your patience, control, and love. You stood on your words.", I tried to console Arjun. But, his tears didn't stand long in his eyes, flying back due to the wind. He tried to wipe them. He knew mom was waiting for him at home.

"Nothing is needed now.", she said.

"Good. Thank you. This is time for us to give him space for sometime.", I appreciated her for her spot-on instincts.

NOVEMBER 29, 9:15 PM, ARJUN'S HOME...

Arjun's left foot opened the motorbike's stand. He opened the door and walked towards his room.

"Arjun, where are you going without eating?"

"Maa... I had some food. You eat and sleep. We shall talk tomorrow.", he said to mom. Arjun rushed to his table without a second thought. The wooden table was covered with a greyish-black table cloth which had a row of novels and piles of books. He picked one of those books with his left hand. A diary of his own thoughts, feelings, and emotions that sailed in it. He named it 'THE INSIGHTS OF THE INSIDE TALKS'. He picked his favorite black ink pen and started to write.

"I've been asking the distance,
to shower some kindness,
I've been asking the time,
to bring me some shine,
I've been asking my life,
to gift me your love.
Today, all of them came to me, as one,
in the form of you, after one long year."

"No distance, No time and No life can break us apart, Anu. I'll be waiting for you."

His little tear drops fell on the book, spreading the black ink. Maybe they told about the darkness he would be in, without Anu.

He turned to the next page.

"Thank you bud! You have been a great ally. Convey my thanks to your ally as well. People often forget your value. If I don't value when I have you, there isn't any need to value you, when I lose you. Today, if you weren't a part of my thought process, the whole day would have been different. Totally different. Be it support, prompts, cautions, confidence and composure, you were with me every milli-second. I'm blessed to be gifted with you. Today, for the first time in the world I thank my *brain* from the bottom of my heart for being my true ally!"

I had never expected him nor seen any either, who'd thank one's own brain. He put down his pen, closed the book and relaxed in his chair gazing at the light yellowish wall. Memories flashed. Eyes dived into sleep.

That day, I was proud, glad and emotional, being a brain for a man of emotions and value. One who valued his own allies, his own brain. Who cares about time for self introductions when a man turns the moments you want, into memories?

I work restlessly, optimizing and personalizing Arjun. He knows well that I was like water which could take the shape of any vessel. He knows that I transform better with positive inputs and turn out worse with the negative ones.

As Arjun said, I shared his heartful thanks to my ally, 'The Gut Bacteria', a microbiome by herself in Arjun's stomach. Gut bacteria are microbes present in every human which guide me, the brain to intake certain food. The food one takes, affects the brain, there-by affects the way one thinks and vice-versa. Maybe that's one of the reasons why people say 'Gut feeling'. She is quite similar to me.

Good bacteria grow if one eats healthy food and bad one grows if one consumes the unhealthier ones.

Mom gets all the appreciation for giving him, feeding him and nurturing him with good food which made the good bacteria evolve and there-by developed Arjun and I to think right. Arjun had gone through me and my ally during his 4-day exam preparation and that's when Arjun and I got closer as he studied me, understood me and the way I worked.

All that needed was some attention!

His name is *Arjun* and yes, 'I' am his *brain, who* drives his thoughts. 'SHE' is the *Gut bacteria,* my one true ally!

INSIGHTS OF THE INSIDE TALKS

PRITAM

"We all live once, so I want to leave an everlasting imprint in people's heart as well as their bookshelves. I don't want to inspire, just want to write and not dissolve into an oblivion!" ~ Pritam

Regarded as the 'King of Darkness' due to the recherche facet his writings have. Fantasy and Horror fictions are his 'claim to fame' genres because his thought process and writing skill is best enunciated through them! 'How to retire at the age of 25' is one of his stratagems in the field of writing, with a couple of anthologies along the way.

Follow him on Instagram - @pritam_himself

I was adopted finally!

I was over the moon to know that someone wanted me and that feeling of belongingness put me into my peaceful void. For years, I craved for the love, care, attention and nurture that most kids got but with a destiny like mine, dreams and desires are not easy to attain in life. But the few years of trial was over when Kalpana aunty and Sanjay uncle accepted me into their life as their son because no one really adopts an orphan who lives under a flyover but they did. They said that I resembled their son, who had passed away although they did not disclose the reason behind his untimely demise and I too was not bothered because for me what was important was I was getting a family. They brought me to their home, which became my home too, just like they promised.

The first time, I stepped into the house, the place was pretty much isolated for 2 people to live in but that thought was out the window, when I saw how huge it was from within. Classic cream distempered walls with aesthetic paintings and picturesque images. Both of them gave me a tour of most parts of the house so that I don't wander off and get lost. Both of them took me to my room and once I opened the door, amazed would be an understatement of what I was feeling. Firstly, I was getting my own room, which was a huge deal in itself but what a perfect room it was. In the right corner of the squarish room, my bed was placed which looked like it was made of some really expensive wood. Right next to it was the bedside table which had a night lamp on it and diagonally opposite to it, was my study table with some accessories to complete its look. My wardrobe was built into the wall and the entire floor was covered with a worn out black carpet.

All in all, it was a dream and I felt it would vanish in a blink of an eye so I cherished each and every nook and corner of the room.

I remembered something, that I had noticed while they were giving me a tour of the house. I hesitated a lot before popping the question, fearing that they will get mad but my mouth had already run off.

"Kalpana aunty, you have not put up any picture of your son. Is there any reason why?" After asking the question, I already regretted it a lot. Both of them glanced at each other, then Kalpana aunty replied, "Well…. we don't display pictures of the dead."

After pausing for a minute she said, "And call me mummy from today, not aunty."

Her words held a different emotion and meaning which made me contented and my spontaneous action at that very instant was to hug her tight. She hugged me back with that same intensity and then kissed me on my forehead, I felt a strange, unknown feeling coursing through my veins. Nobody had ever kissed me like this before, leaving behind such a sensation.

"Go and take a bath!", she suggested. "And throw these, we have many clothes for you kept in your wardrobe."

I went inside the bathroom, which felt like another room to me. I was amazed by the mosaic design on the tiled wall. Anyways, I showered and cleaned myself with the soaps and shampoos so much that I couldn't even recognise myself at first. Well, when I came out of the bathroom, I saw a set of clothes were kept on my bed. I put them on, combed my hair like a *saheb* and went straight into the kitchen, where mummy was chopping some vegetables for our dinner.

"Do you eat meat?", she asked, smiling when she saw me.

"I do, but I never had much"

"Don't worry, here you can have as much as you want", Papa said as he entered in the kitchen.

"Give me some meat from the freezer", she said. "Today, I'll make some meat for my boy".

He opened the chest freezer and gave her a packet full of red meat. Meanwhile, I was standing there, glancing at both of them simultaneously and continuously thanking God for giving me more than what I prayed for.

Papa took me again on a small tour of the house, rooms that I had not seen then. They had a hobby room which had a piano, two guitars, lots of books and a pair of sofas, in which you can sit and enjoy every book you want.

"Do you know how to play this?", I was awe-struck looking at the piano.

"Umm… A bit"

"Will you teach me?"

"I'd love to"

My life turned upside down in a flash. Just a few hours ago, I was an eleven year old boy who lived under the flyover, begged for his living, trying desperately to make ends meet and now I was not anymore. I had a roof over my head, food on a plate, clothes on my body and most importantly, a family to cherish and love.

Soon, it was dinner time and Papa took me back to the dining room. Rice, chapati, meat, curry, salads, raita and sweets were all I could see on the table. This is definitely more than what I used to have when I was on the streets. More than hungry, I was excited to eat my dinner using cutlery but I was in a dilemma of what to eat first – rice or chapati? Mummy must have noticed my hesitation and helped me make a decision by serving me some rice first, on which she put the curry and meat. It looked absolutely delicious and the aroma was brewing through the air. I picked up my spoon, nervous as hell to dug into my rice. But I horribly failed at using the spoon and had some rice escape the plate because of that. Very slowly, I replaced the spoon with my hand and started mixing the rice with the curry. Once the first morsel touched my tongue, I was in seventh heaven of delight. This was the best curry I had ever had and the meat was tender and juicy. Even in a lifetime, I would have never imagined that I would get to eat an amazing meal to my heart's content. Papa and Mummy had smiles on their face when they saw me relishing on the meat.

It was 10 o'clock and unlike the streets, that meant bedtime. I was sitting on the bed when Mummy took out a quilt while Papa turned on the AC for me. Mummy asked me to lie down and she covered me with the quilt like I'm her own little baby.

"Good night, Raju", she tenderly said and kissed me on my cheek. I felt a little bit of saliva on my cheek, which I definitely ignored.

"I'm keeping the water bottle here" Papa placed the bottle on the bedside table. "…if you feel thirsty you don't need to go anywhere."

"Can I ask something, to the both of you?", I asked thoughtfully.

"Sure", Mummy said.

"I don't like being called—Raju", I said. "So, can I change my name?"

"Sure", she replied after looking at papa. "Umm… how about… Raj?"

"Raj is nice", I said happily.

"Well, then Raj Sharma. Good Night", she said.

"Good night, Raj", he said and they walked out of the room, closing the door behind them.

I thanked God again for everything and started thinking about the nightlife on the streets. Car horns, lights, drunkards and so many elements that never let me sleep this early so, it was evident that my habits are not going away so soon as I still couldn't sleep at least until the midnight.

I was sitting in my room when a boy, same age as mine, walked in. He was wearing the same t-shirt that I wore after taking the shower. He came close to me and said, "Get out". I wanted to ask who he was and how he had come in but all I could say was "No". He was continuously saying the same thing and I was also murmuring the same, until he screamed, "GET OUT". It was so loud that it felt like my eardrums were about to explode.

I woke up with a jolt, I was panting and that voice still echoing in my ears, the dream was too real and I couldn't shake off the uncomfortable feeling I had gotten from it. I looked at the clock in the yellow dim night light and it was half-past two, the room was freezing and I was shivering because of the AC. I picked up the remote and turned it around, trying to figure out how it worked. Once I had figured it out, I picked up the water bottle from the bedside table and drank some water. I once again lay down on the bed, pulling the quilt over me and stared at the ceiling, still reeling from the dream I had seen. Soon, I had fallen asleep because of the comfy quilt and the dream did not return, thankfully.

Next morning, I woke up and walked out of the room. I found Mummy in the kitchen; she was making something for our breakfast.

"Good morning", she smiled as she saw me. "You woke up early"

"I woke up late today actually." I said. "Usually I wake up at 5, because of the cars and all."

"Go, freshen up. I'm making sandwiches for you.", she chuckled.

I rushed to the bathroom, cleaned myself real quick and ran back to the table. Mummy served a glass full of milk and some sandwiches as I sat on the chair. While eating, I was constantly pondering about the dream I saw last night. Lost in my thoughts, I didn't realise that I had stopped eating. Papa noticed this and asked me, pointing towards the sandwiches.

"Isn't it good?"

"No, it's… delicious, Papa."

"Then why aren't you eating?", Mummy asked. "Is everything okay?"

"Yeah… I just want to ask you something?"

She nodded, indicating me to go on.

"Whose t-shirt am I wearing?", I asked, looking into her eyes.

She exchanged looks with papa that clearly expressed that I had asked a question that she didn't want to answer.

"Well…", Papa exhaled. "It's Sameer's t-shirt."

"Sameer?"

"Our son, who died three years ago in an accident. He was of your age…" Mummy said. "We didn't tell you the whole story, because we don't talk about him and we want to start a new life with you."

As she finished, a drop of tear rolled down her cheek which she wiped and walked towards her room without eating another bite. I wanted to stop her but papa stopped me by saying "Let's leave her alone for some time". I wanted to go but I also did not want to make things worse.

"Why did you ask that?", he asked after a while.

"Just like that… I didn't have any intention of hurting her", I lied.

I was feeling guilty of raising the topic of their son's death. She brought me here, gave me their name, gave me a new life and what I gave her in return—sorrow. These thoughts were making me feel worse, I wanted to apologize but papa asked me to leave her alone. I was lying down and thinking about mummy the whole time until she came to call me for lunch. I hugged her and apologized, and as expected she forgave me. I also promised her that I would never talk about him.

The nights were starting out to be normal for me, but I still couldn't sleep until midnight. So, out of curiosity, I got out of bed and sat on the chair in front of the study table. It had a lamp, a notebook and a pen stand that had all sorts of pens. I grabbed one, opened the notebook and tried to doodle something. After a few minutes, I got bored and I walked towards the cupboard, I held the handles and opened it. The same boy, from the previous night, was sitting inside the cupboard, staring into my eyes. I froze for a second and fell down on the floor. I started to scream, crawling out of the room. My screams woke up Papa who rushed out of his room and came running towards me.

"What happened?", Papa asked.

"He's... he's in there", I was panting heavily now.

"Who's there?", he asked looking at the door of my room.

"Sa... Sameer", I choked.

"Sameer?", he took his name, as if he had heard it for the very first time.

I nodded slowly.

"Our son, Sameer?" It was like he had just realised that he had a son.

"Yes. He's inside the cupboard."

"What happened?" Mummy also came out of the room now.

I looked at her and her innocent oval face had reminded me of the promise I made.

"Come with me!", he said and started walking towards my room.

I followed him into the room. I was still very terrified and running away was the best option at that very moment. The doors of my wardrobe were shut, which was strange because I don't remember shutting them while consumed by my fear. Papa opened the cupboard but alas, there was no one inside. He looked at me, 'I think you are crazy' look graced his face. On reading his expression, I kept quiet because I did not want to anger him anymore. He walked out of my room, clearly very disappointed by my actions and closed the door behind him. I climbed into my bed and stuffed myself under the quilt. I kept staring at the ceiling and before I even knew it, I had already fallen asleep.

Next morning, I woke up late, like really late. I walked into the bathroom, took a bath and slowly went to the table for breakfast. I heard some noise coming from the kitchen. So, I went to see and I saw Mummy standing, chopping some red meat with a butcher's knife. The blade of the knife was covered with dried blood and frost meat. She got startled as she saw me standing there, staring at her.

"Oh my God! You scared me."

"Sorry!"

"Have you had your breakfast?"

"No. I was just going to right now.", I said and walked back to the table.

I was still pondering over what I saw last night and just thinking about it was giving me the chills and shivers. My thoughts were broken by the ringing of the doorbell. I got up to open the door but Mummy beat me to it as she rushed out of the kitchen. She came back followed by Papa who was holding multiple bags of groceries. He handed her the bags and sat next to me, grave silence engulfing the room.

"I thought you went to your office, Papa?"

"I'm on leave today." he replied dryly.

"Sorry for yesterday."

He kept quiet, without any expressions gracing his features, which made me more anxious and sad.

The day got over really fast with nothing significant that happened, and so did the night. After having dinner, I went into my room and climbed into my bed. In a blink of an eye, I was out like a light. And there I was — again, sitting on my bed when I saw him, Sameer walking towards me. I wanted to run, scream and shout but this time, I could do none of them, it was as if I had become paralyzed due to fear. He came really close and sat beside me, staring at me intensely. I was terrified of looking at his face but I couldn't resist the urge and when I did, I saw absolute pain, sorrow and anguish in his eyes. His eyes told a different story altogether, which made me wonder what did he mean by 'Get Out!'. He suddenly stood up from the bed, walked towards the table and caressed the table fondly but the soft expression on his face changed as soon as he touched the cupboard. He turned towards me and yelled loudly "GET OUT!". Frightened out of my wits, I woke up with a jerk, sweat covered my face and body glistening in the dark and my erratic breathing had shot off the roof. What was he trying to tell me? After that nightmare, I couldn't sleep at all, fearing that he might return again.

It was soon morning and I reluctantly dragged myself to the bathroom. After cleaning myself, I walked to the kitchen and I was shell-shocked to see Mummy looking very happy while cleaning the utensils. Sensing her good mood, I didn't mention about Sameer and the nightmare. As I was wondering where Papa was, Papa walked out of the hobby room, holding a book in his hand. After a lot of deliberation, I spoke up.

"Papa", I said. "Can we go out, today?"

"Well, we'd love to but not today"

I wanted to go out as it had been three days and I had been confined to the four walls of this house which was extremely strange as I had never been in a house for very long. But I didn't want to upset them anymore so I just sat silent with my head lowered. After completing my breakfast, I went to my room and bolted it from inside as I wanted to be alone, and for the first time, I was missing the street, the cars, the blaring of the horns. I wanted to go back to the streets but it felt like I would never get to see those streets again. I was sitting on the bed when I heard a scratching sound coming from the cupboard. I stood up and walked towards the cupboard weighing each step I made, a cold chill ran down my spine, but I still dared to swalk towards the cupboard, held the handles with my shaking hands and opened the doors at once.

There was nothing inside the cupboard and mysteriously, the scratching sound had also stopped. I closed the cupboard doors and returned back to my bed. I lay down and stared at the ceiling, thinking about the dream, more like nightmare, that I had witnessed in the last three days.

The day droned away somehow and at the dinner table, I prodded them about my academics for which they replied with a smile, "Don't worry, we have planned *everything*"

I didn't understand what they meant and it did sound kind of fishy, so to change the topic I said, "I was hoping to have meat today."

"Meat is finished", Papa replied nonchalantly.

"Yeah. But we'll *eat* that tomorrow!" Mummy reassured.

After dinner, I went back to my safe haven, my room followed by mummy who came in like every other day to tuck me in. But that day she brought a glass of milk for me, which was something new. She handed me the glass and asked me to drink it, without any questions to which I obeyed her like a good boy. She turned on the AC and covered me with the quilt and I could feel my eyes were getting heavy—almost immediately. Mummy kissed me on my forehead and instead of her usual kiss, it felt like she licked my forehead. I couldn't think much about it because I was very drowsy and soon, I was out like a light.

I woke up because of the noise around me and when I opened my eyes, I had a blurry vision at first. Once my vision became coherent, I saw Mummy and Papa talking to each other in loud whispers.

"Mummy!", I called her.

She looked at me and turned to papa and said, "I knew the medicine will not be enough, but you were so confident. Now look, he's already awake!"

"Mummy!" I wanted to get up but I couldn't. My whole body was numb, I wasn't even able to move my fingers. What is happening to me?! Why couldn't I move?!

Papa said something to her which was barely audible to me. Mummy then went towards the cupboard, grabbed the black carpet by the corner, folded it and pulled the cupboard to create a small space but before I could understand what she was doing, Papa blocked my vision. He lifted me up in his arms and turned around. For the first time since I got here, I noticed the multiple skid marks on the floor which was evidently made by the constant pushing and pulling of the cupboard. I was stunned to see a secret gateway appearing right behind the cupboard. Mummy went in followed by Papa, with me in his arms, and no clarity in whatsoever was going on.

It was dark in there until Mummy turned on the lights and there we were, standing in an almost empty but suspiciously clean room. It was completely different from the rest of the house. It had a stretcher right in the middle of the room, a chair and a small metal cupboard in the corner. The walls and the floor were covered with shiny white tiles and two drains could be seen inbuilt. I looked around and I saw a board hanging on the left wall with pictures of many children pinned up to it. I even saw a picture of their own son Sameer pinned up among those pictures. He put me down on the chair and went towards the cupboard. My body was back to being normal and I was able to move normally.

"Mummy, why are we here? And what is this place?", I asked.

"Well, we'll have a party here!" the innocence that was always there, had disappeared from her face and she clicked a picture of mine on her smartphone.

"Why Sameer's picture is here?"

"Where is he?", she asked like she had never seen him before or heard of him.

I pointed at the picture in the board and they burst into laughter like I cracked the funniest joke they could ever think of.

"We never had any child", she said "and that boy was just another one like you"

"What do you mean?"

"Well, he and the others on that board were our *food*!", Papa replied while turning towards me with a bone saw in his hands. "Just like you're going to be"

"What!" I was about to get up but Mummy held me from the back. I kept struggling against her hold but she was a lot stronger and bigger than I thought. I was mentally pleading and hoping that all of this was a nightmare or maybe a joke. But once, Papa plugged in the bone saw and checked whether or not it was working properly, the whirring sound from the bone saw broke my reverie of thoughts.

"How? How can you eat humans?", I asked in a disgusted tone.

"Well, we are delicious, aren't we?", Mummy replied, licking my ear from the back, sending a shiver down my nape. "… and don't talk like *you* haven't eaten them."

"I? You mean the meat was of—"

"Yes, it was of your so-called *Sameer*", she laughed.

Papa came very close to me and just as he was about to cut my head off, without any second thoughts, I kicked him in his groin so hard that the saw fell from his hands and he collapsed, writhing in pain. Mummy slapped me and I fell off the chair. She immediately rushed towards Papa to help him up. He was groaning in pain because of the solid kick and one thing I was sure of was that he was not going to get up for a while. Meanwhile, I got up and tried to run but Mummy was quick on her feet, running towards with a surgical blade. When she plunged at me, I stepped back which was a wrong move on my part because now she was blocking the entrance with the death weapon in her hand. Sensing my helplessness and misery, she grabbed that opportunity and charged at me. I ran towards the stretcher and while running, I pulled it behind me unconsciously to dodge her. But that worked in my favour because she slipped and fell down on the floor. The surgical blade got lodged in her throat making her choke and cough up blood as she struggled to remove the blade. Just as she removed the blade, she was gone. Seeing her laying lifeless in her blood, Papa cried out her name loudly in attempts of waking her up but she was gone. Her blood was slowly flushing down the drains and looking at the drains, I realized that it could have been my blood if I wouldn't have reacted on my instinct. When I looked at Papa, I saw that he was slowly getting up, even though he was in tremendous amount of pain and coming towards me, revenge glaring in his eyes. I looked around to see whether there was something that I could use to save myself but clearly, it was a very deserted room. Papa slowly cornered me into the wall and when I tried to kick again, he dodged it and grasped my arm. I kept jerking my hand but his hold became tighter with every struggle I put across. I held the corner of the stretcher in hopes of not being pulled across the room but instead, the stretcher was moving with me and soon I felt a loose screw unhinge from one end. That was my chance! I grabbed hold of it and with all the energy left, I pierced it into his left eye. Blood spurted out of his eye and he bellowed in pain. He let my arm free and fell down on the floor, screaming and thrashing in affliction. I grabbed my opportunity and ran as fast as I could, not looking back even for a second. I closed the doors of the cupboard and locked my room so that they couldn't escape in anyway. I grabbed the keys from the shelf, unlocked the gates and ran to the nearest police station.

My tattered clothes with blood stains on them was enough evidence for them to know that something terrible had happened. I recounted all the details of my torture, the people who I thought loved me, the house and the cupboard. They filed a case and asked me to take them to that house. I guided them to that location where they found both the bodies. Mummy was found to be lying in her blood but a policeman said that papa died because his skull was fractured, which I never saw happening. After the house was searched, they retrieved some tools from the cupboard, these tools were used to amputate humans. It was the last time I stepped into that house.

But,

It has been fifteen years since then and those memories still give me the goosebumps. I wake up each night, sweating excessively with an irregular pulse rate because of reliving nightmares where I am getting eaten alive. They did die for good but it still often feels like they — Mummy and Papa, are still looking at me as their unfinished meal.

KAVAN PURANIK

"I am just a mere writer, who writes for fun!" ~ Kavan Puranik

An Engineering student, whose passion spiked up when he was just a mere child. Ah, an empty page for him evokes a desire so great that he is possessed and he wants to fill it with words, words that tell stories of what could have been and what can be, stories of monsters, magic and madness, stories that only he can tell. Sci-fi and Magical Realism are the two genres that intrigues him when writing micro-fictions and short stories.

Follow him on Instagra - @the_tavern_of_tales

What are you afraid of?

It's finally that time of the year. The time of the year that makes the rest of the insufferable year sufferable. The time of the year that comes like a breath of fresh air to a drowning man (or woman). You run towards the waves and leap into the water striking (what you think is) a cool pose. You're drenched from head to toe and enjoy every moment of it. Your brother on the other hand is on the beach, building sand castles. Your dad's taking pictures of him while your mom is getting a tan. Your beloved dog Iggy follows you into the water. You are having the time of your life!

The wind grows colder all of a sudden. Out of nowhere, storm clouds envelop the sky. Bright lightning illuminates the horizon, the brightest you've ever seen. The thunder that came after was deafening. The beach gets shrouded in an eerie darkness. You notice people frantically screaming and running away from the water. For a moment, you freeze like a deer in front of headlights but run like your life depends on it after coming back to your senses.

In this confusion, Iggy is separated from you. You struggle to find your parents. Your eyes are filled with tears and dread as you call out to them. The water slows your pace as you attempt to run out of it. You then spot your parents running towards you from the other side of the beach. As you excitedly wave at them, hoping to hear them say "It's alright son, you'll be okay" like they always did whenever you were in trouble, a volley of spikes the size of pencils, hit them on their face. They just died! In addition to the lives of your parents, the spikes claim several other lives. It was now clear what people were running from, if it wasn't quite clear before.

You freeze, unwilling to accept a reality that is indeed stranger than your wildest flights of fantasy. A cold chill runs down your spine followed by an outburst of angry and terrified screams. After a few seconds, a monstrous roar from the sea amplified the panic and chaos. A slimy creature with a huge eye emerges from the sea. A huge tentacle comes out of the water followed by another volley of spikes. This time, some of the spikes hit you, one of them punctures the skin on your right arm, one of them nearly takes your ear off, one of them hits your left shoulder. You're in a world of pain, but you try to get away nonetheless.

You then spot a helpless little girl crying, she hurt her ankle but what's worse, she's severely traumatized, the next wave of spikes would surely kill her.

From the other side, you hear a dog whimpering, it's Iggy! both his hind legs were hurt and a part of his tail was cut off, he was bleeding. You notice the tentacle moving towards your general direction, you want to help both the girl and Iggy, but you only have the time and energy to save one of them.

If you want to save Iggy, turn to page 254

If you want to save the little girl, turn to page 252

You decide to fight violence with violence.

You pick up the rod and charge towards the tentacle, yelling battle cries that made sense only to you, the memories of all the deaths in the beach still fresh in your mind. Your sorrow now turned into resent, your fear turned into fury! You start thrashing the tentacle furiously, driving it back an inch. You even manage to draw some blood near it's slimy tip. You then feel something coarse wrap around your neck, you turn back. There are a dozen more tentacles behind you. Before you can react, they lift you off the ground and wrap themselves around your arms and legs. The rod you are holding falls off your hands. Their grip grows tighter and tighter until your arms and legs are crushed, but they leave your head untouched.

One of the tentacles picks up the metal rod and begin swinging it at you with the same vigour that you exhibited earlier. With each blow, you feel your consciousness slip further away from you. Soon, everything was a blur. You felt immense pain when the barrage of blows began, but now... You feel nothing!

THE END

You run for your life!
"Oh god! What have I done to deserve this???"

You try to run as far away from the water as you possibly can. As you run, tentacles keep popping up all around you, some of them even graze you a bit. But you keep running! Soon the tentacles stop following you. You stood on higher ground now, you could see what's going on in the beach. It was a horrendous sight! There are dead bodies everywhere, the sand coloured red with blood, corpses covered with spikes, and now, the owner of the tentacles arose from the dark sea, it's ravenous face momentarily visible as lightning struck. The phantasmal sight sent a cold chill down your spine.

"What's happening? Why is this happening?"

It's not something you thought you'd see, not in your wildest dreams, not even in your scariest nightmares. You think of going to the police and telling them what happened. You manage to tear your gaze away from that dreadful sight and turn back. To your surprise, you see nothing, absolutely nothing, just complete darkness.

"What's going on?" you break into a cold sweat, *"Am I dead?"*

You hear someone giggling. You turn your head in random directions to find the source of the noise.

"Hello there, oni chan" says the voice of a little girl, she stood right next to you, it's the same little girl whom you abandoned at the beach. Her voice startles you. You fall off your feet as you let out a loud gasp. You soon recover your balance, but not your composure.

"What are you afraid of?" She asks.

"E..E..Excuse me?", you stutter.

"What are you afraid of?"

"I'm sorry for abandoning you like that, I should have come to save you, I'm really sorry", you eyes were filled with tears.

"Wouldn't have ended well, what are you afraid of?"

"You're a ghost aren't you? You're trying to punish me for something I did"

She smiled. "No, what are you afraid of?"

"Then how are you alive? I saw you die, who are you? What are you?"

"What are you afraid of?"

Your eyes widen, you feel a cold chill run down your spine, without saying a word, you run away from her, as fast as you can. You try your best to get away from her, but you hear her giggling again. "What are you afraid of?"

"Why do you keep repeating that? What do you want?"

She chuckled, "What are you afraid of?"

"Okay, now it's getting annoying, is any of this real? Am I dreaming?"

She chuckled again, "What are you afraid of?"

"Where is my family? Is Iggy a demon too? Where are we?"

"You're asking the wrong questions, what are you afraid of?"

You kept quiet for a while, it appears that the more questions you ask, the harder it is for you to get away from her.

"Maybe the only way to escape this ... Whatever this is, is to answer the question"

"What do I do to get out of here?", You ask.

"What are you afraid of?"

If you're afraid of Sharks, go to page 257

If you're afraid of Centipedes, go to page 256

If you want to ask more questions, turn to page 253

With all the speed you can muster, you run towards the little girl.

"Hey!!", you cry out, "Get out of there!!!"

You see the tentacle drawing near, it's a lot faster than you thought it was. You reach the girl, you try to help her up, but then you notice something strange...

You see something wrapped around her leg, a smaller tentacle! It held on to her firmly, anchoring her to the ground. You try your best to break it free but the tentacle has spikes, your hands are now bleeding. It was a trap!

"Help us!!!" you yell.

Your voice is lost in the mortified screams of a fleeing crowd on the brink of madness. It's too late for anything now! Before you even get a chance to say goodbye to this cruel world, the tentacle grabs you both, crushing your neck in the process and killing you. It drags both your corpses into the water.

THE END

"What are YOU afraid of?", you ask.

The demon's mischievous smile disappeared. Her face wore a scared expression, "You" she said, and then she was gone.

You feel something wet touching your feet. You look down. The ground you were standing on now became water. The darkness faded now and in it's place, you could see a familiar location. The beach looked normal now, like it did before anything happened. Your body begins to transform into something you couldn't recognize. You see yourself playing in the beach, you see your parents, your brother and Iggy, but you're not with them. You're standing on top of the sea, miles away from the beach. As soon as you realize that, you slowly start sinking.

"Help! Help!" You shout as you sink deeper, splashing your arms and legs wildly. Soon your voice disappears and in it's place, you hear a monstrous roar. Your vision is now limited, you can't feel your hands or legs, but you feel something else in it's place. A lot of somethings. You were choking a bit in the beginning, but now you could breathe just fine. You take a good look at yourself.

"Noooooooooooo" you say, but instead of words, a monstrous roar comes out, the monstrous roar of a kraken.

THE END

With a heavy heart, you abandon the girl and approach Iggy.

"Iggy!!!!" you yell, "Here boy!!!"

As you slowly make your way towards your beloved dog, the tentacle grabs the little girl and drag her into the water. Iggy starts barking uncontrollably and wags whatever's left of his tail. You reach Iggy, but after a failed attempt at picking him up, you realize that you don't have the strength required to pick up a fully grown golden retriever. Soon, another wave of spikes is launched from one of the tentacles. This time, you thought you were done for, you lay on the sand, hugging your beloved dog Iggy, waiting for it all to end.

To your surprise, every single spike misses you! What luck! You feel Iggy's collar heat up. You then notice Iggy biting your shirt. He was up on all four! Iggy somehow carried you on his back and took you to one of the stores; away from the monster, for the moment at least. Iggy began licking your wounds. To your surprise, all your wounds heal along with a few injuries and scars! Your physical ones that is. You now had some time to register what went on out there. You bawl like a baby, your losses are tremendous. You were not ready to deal with death yet, especially not a grotesque slaughter such as this. Iggy rested his face on your lap, trying his best to console you. To a certain extent, it worked.

It took a while for your mind to regain it's sanity. Even though despair clouded your thoughts, you begin to question the strange events occurring around you. Even with all that is happening, some things didn't quite add up.

"How did my wounds heal? How did Iggy's legs heal? What's happening?!!" You felt so helpless.

"Your brother might still be alive" a voice said.

It startled you.

Iggy gets up from your lap. "I need to save little Jimmy", he said.

 "You can talk? My dog can talk!" you say, "Aaargh! Why's this happening to me?? What's going on?"

"Please calm down, I'll go get him, keep this with you, in case I don't return" Iggy gave you his collar and whined like a puppy.

"I'll miss you". With that, he left.

You momentarily ruminate about the monster, the talking dog, the massacre you witnessed and what it all meant in the grand scheme of things until a tentacle, that looked like a miniature version of the big ones, popped out from underneath the shop. Your first instinct was to get out of there, but you remembered the horrendous happenings outside, you then see a sharp metal rod next to you. It could be used as a weapon.

If you want to pick up the sharp piece of metal, turn to page 248

If you want to run, turn to page 249

"Centipedes" you say.

The little girl smiles at you and disappears. The sand beneath your feet felt different. You look down.

"AAÀAAH!"

Every grain of sand was replaced by a centipede! You try to run away but you don't know where to go. The more you ran, the more centipedes you disturbed. One by one, they start biting you. At one point, you were bitten so much that you couldn't stand anymore. You fall down flat on your face, the centipedes swarm all over you, crawling over your hands, your back, your hair and every part of your body that you can think of. Some of them even entered your clothes. Some parts of your body went numb whereas others hurt like hell. You try not to shout lest the centipedes enter your mouth, but the centipedes enter your mouth anyway.

"Are centipedes carnivorous?" were your last thoughts as the centipedes ate you alive... from the inside out.

THE END

"Sharks" you say.

The little girl laughs hysterically and disappears, but the darkness remains. The only way to go is forward. At this point, you decided to abide by the new reality that you found yourself in. You walk towards the beach with one goal in mind: Destroy the monster. You have no idea how to do it, but you keep moving forward.

A ray of sunlight penetrates the darkness, followed immediately by another and then another. From the horizon, you see an army of sharks charging towards the monster. They moved towards the shark in speeds you didn't think was possible. There is something peculiar about these sharks, they have ... saddles. Also, they touched none of the human corpses. The monster launches a volley of spikes and tries thwarting away the army of sharks. Several sharks were hit but many of them marched on or rather swam forward. They cling to the monster's tentacles attempting to bite off several chunks of the monster's flesh.

Another group of sharks completely ignore the tentacles and make their way towards another target. It was almost as if they had intricate battle formations. In a moment, their target became obvious. They were going for the eye, however, none of them succeeded in reaching it. That's where the concentration of the projectile spikes and tentacles were the most, it was impossible to reach there. Soon, smaller tentacles, like the ones from the shop, start to protrude out of the larger ones. These tentacles wrap around the sharks and fling them back into the water. Despite their efforts, the sharks' numbers start dwindling. The sea now turned blood red.

One particular shark is flung towards you. It fell out of the water, struggling to breathe. You want to help it, but you're terrified of Sharks. Maybe it's because of the movies, maybe it's because of their sharp teeth or maybe it's because they are scary creatures in general. Whatever the reason is, nothing frightens you like a shark does. There was a phase in your life when you wouldn't even step into swimming pools because of how scared you were of sharks. However, you can relate to the drowning creature, both of you are deeply wounded (in one way or another) and are clinging to life after losing loved ones. After all that you've been through, you somehow muster up the courage to pull the shark back into the sea, you hop on it's saddle and as the shark begins to move, you pick up one of the stray spikes littered on the beach along with the corpses. As you move towards the creature, just like before, Iggy's collar heats up and the spikes miss you entirely, even the shark's physical wounds begin to heal. The shark dives in and swims towards the monster at full speed. The un-penetrable zone was now penetrable. Without a moment of hesitation, the shark dives into the water and begins swimming upwards as it reaches the un-penetrable zone, you could tell what it was thinking. As the shark sprang up, the creature lashed out it's tentacle. You jump off the shark's saddle and in one swift motion, dodge the tentacle's attack and climb on to it. Since the monster's skin is too slimy, you use the fallen spike to climb up which didn't seem to hurt the monster. The sharks made it look so easy to tear off it's flesh, but to you, it was virtually impossible. You find it difficult to climb up to the eye with all the small tentacles lashing at you. Even though the tentacles missed you, they kept coming back, the closer the call, the hotter Iggy's collar got.

Your target was in sight but it was no cakewalk to actually get there. With every meter you got closer, the ferocity of the attacks became more intense. You couldn't attack with the spike because you need that to stay on the tentacle, you felt Iggy's collar losing heat. Eventually, the tentacles wouldn't miss. You crouch down holding the spike and begin to think. This position only made you more vulnerable though. You never had great concentration ability, but now your life depended on it. Then, you get up, with a gleam in your eyes that says, "I'm gonna end this man's whole career".

As soon as one of the tentacles tries to grab, you let go of the spike, with your arms spread out, you fall to your death but just before you hit the ocean floor, a shark cushions your fall and dives underneath, the shark seems to be moving according to your will, "just as I thought, you say". You stayed underwater for as long as you could, waiting for the right moment to strike. When you're almost out of breath, the two of you shoot up, you manage to see the eye. With all your strength, you thrust the spike into the monster's eye. Your determination to kill the beast combined with your urge to hold on to something in order to break your fall was just enough to penetrate the eye. The monster let out another scary roar, but this time, a roar of pain. The creature thrashed around more wildly than ever before till the moment leading up to it's death, and then it fell. So did you. It appears that your luck had run out at some point during the jump, your legs are bloody, there is one spike lodged into your other leg. There are cuts and bruises all over your body. You keep sinking into the depths until you're engulfed by water and darkness. You can't breathe. Before your eyes closed, you saw something coming towards you, you couldn't discern what it was.

When your eyes open, you're blinded by a surge of bright light. You find it difficult to comprehend your surroundings. When your vision returns to normal, you see Iggy and a familiar face looking at you.

"Jimmy!", you hug your little brother, tears rolling down from your eyes.

"I was so scared! I-I-" he said.

"It's okay now, the scary monster's gone … and so is everybody else" there is a hint of sadness in your tone.

"Not everyone" says a female voice. It startles you.

"What the?-" you say "What are you doing here? What do you want?"

"It's alright" said Iggy, "She means us no harm"

"Nothing's alright Iggy" you say with tears forming in your eyes "Everything's gone!"

"It could have been a lot worse" says Iggy.

"Iggy can talk!" says Jimmy, still hugging you.

"I know, Jimmy" you say.

"Where did you find him?" you ask Iggy.

"A tale for another time" he said.

Jimmy lets go of his embrace and asks. "Where's mommy and Daddy?"

You try your best to hold back the tears and be strong for the sake of your little brother, still you turn away, finding it difficult to look him in the eye.

"They ..." you try to pull yourself together, "told us to wait here, they'll come find us"

The little girl started laughing maniacally.

You look at the horizon, the sky is painted in hues of orange, yellow and red. It is the most beautiful sunset you have ever seen, but also the saddest. Even Jimmy gazed into the distance as he sat beside you, lost in the beauty of the vista before him. Iggy sat beside you, licking your face. The little girl giggles and sits down beside Jimmy. All of you sit amid the corpses of the dearly departed and watch the sun set on this dreary day.

THE END

Thanks for being a part of this journey!

You are free to unbuckle your seatbelts

And

Your minds are free to wander